GOLDERS GREEN LIBRARY

KT-559-459

THE
SIREN

30131 05388140 2

LONDON BOROUGH OF BARNET

Also by
KIERA CASS
The Selection
The Elite
The One
The Heir
Happily Ever After: Companion to the Selection Series

THE
SIREN

KIERA CASS

HarperCollins*Publishers*

First published in the USA by HarperTeen,
an imprint of HarperCollins *Publishers* Inc. in 2016
First published in paperback in Great Britain in 2016
by HarperCollins Children's Books,
an imprint of HarperCollins *Publishers* Ltd,
1 London Bridge Street,
London SE1 9GF

www.harpercollins.co.uk

The Siren
Copyright © 2016 by Kiera Cass
All rights reserved.

ISBN: 978-0-00-815793-7

Printed and bound in England by Clays Ltd, St Ives plc
Typography by Sarah Hoy

Kiera Cass asserts the moral right to be identified
as the author of the work.

Conditions of Sale
This book is sold subject to the condition that it shall not,
by way of trade or otherwise, be lent, re-sold, hired out or
otherwise circulated without the publisher's prior written consent
in any form of binding or cover other than that in which it is
published and without a similar condition including this
condition being imposed on the subsequent purchaser.

MIX
Paper from
responsible sources
FSC
www.fsc.org
FSC® C007454

FSC™ is a non-profit international organisation established to promote
the responsible management of the world's forests. Products carrying the
FSC label are independently certified to assure consumers that they come
from forests that are managed to meet the social, economic and
ecological needs of present and future generations,
and other controlled sources.

Find out more about HarperCollins and the environment at
www.harpercollins.co.uk/green

For Liz—

Because she's the kind of girl who songs should be written about, poems should be composed for, and books should be dedicated to

1

It's funny what you hold on to, the things you remember when everything ends. I can still picture the paneling on the walls of our stateroom and recall precisely how plush the carpet was. I remember the saltwater smell, permeating the air and sticking to my skin, and the sound of my brothers' laughter in the other room, like the storm was an exciting adventure instead of a nightmare.

More than any sense of fear or worry, there was an air of irritation hanging in the room. The storm was throwing off our evening's plans; there would be no dancing on the upper deck tonight, no chance to parade around in my new dress. These were the woes that plagued my life then, so insignificant they're almost shameful to own up to. But that was my once upon a time, back when my reality felt like a story because it was so good.

"If this rocking doesn't stop soon, I won't have time to fix my hair before dinner," Mama complained. I peeked up at her from where I was lying on the floor, trying desperately not to throw up. Mama's reflection looked as glamorous as a movie star, and her finger waves seemed perfect to me. But she was never satisfied. "You ought to get off the floor," she continued, glancing down at me. "What if the help comes in?"

I hobbled over to one of the chaise lounges, doing—as always—what I was told, though I didn't think this position was necessarily any more ladylike. I closed my eyes, praying that the water would still. I didn't want to be sick. Our journey up until that final day had been utterly ordinary, just a family trip from point A to point B. I can't remember now where we were heading. What I do recall is that we were, as per usual, traveling in style. We were one of the few lucky families who had survived the Crash with our wealth intact—and Mama liked to make sure people knew it. So we were situated in a beautiful suite with decent-size windows and personal stewards at our beck and call. I was entertaining the idea of ringing for one and asking for a bucket.

It was then, in that bleary haze of sickness, that I heard something, almost like a far-off lullaby. It made me curious and, somehow, thirsty. I lifted my dizzy head and saw Mama turn her attention to the window as well, searching for the sound. Our eyes met for a moment, both of us needing assurance that what we were hearing was real. When we knew we weren't alone, we focused on the window again, listening. The music was intoxicatingly beautiful, like a hymn to the devout.

Papa leaned into the room, his neck sporting a fresh bandage where he'd cut himself trying to shave during the storm. "Is that the band?" he asked. His tone was calm, but the desperation in his eyes was haunting

"Maybe. It sounds like it's coming from outside, doesn't it?" Mama was suddenly breathless and eager, one hand on her neck as she swallowed excitedly. "Let's go see." She hopped up and grabbed her sweater. I was shocked. She hated being in the rain.

"But Mama, your makeup. You just said—"

"Oh, that," she said, brushing me off and shrugging her arms into an ivory cardigan. "We'll only be gone a moment. I'll have time to fix it when we get back."

"I think I'll stay." I was just as drawn to the music as the rest of them, but the clammy feeling on my face reminded me how close I was to being sick. Leaving our room couldn't be a good idea in my state, and I curled up a little tighter, resisting the urge to stand up and follow.

Mama turned back and met my eyes. "I'd feel better if

you were by my side," she said with a smile.

Those were my mother's last words to me.

Even as I opened my mouth to protest, I found myself standing up and crossing the cabin to follow her. It wasn't just about obeying anymore. I had to get up on deck. I had to be closer to the song. If I had stayed in our room, I probably would have been trapped and gone down with the ship. Then I could have joined my family. In heaven or hell, or in nowhere, if it was all a lie. But no.

We went up the stairs, joined along the way by scores of other passengers. It was then I knew something was wrong. Some of the passengers were rushing, fighting their way through the masses, while others looked like they were sleepwalking.

I stepped into the thrashing rain, pausing just outside the threshold to take in the scene. Pressing my hands over my ears to shut out the crashing thunder and hypnotic music, I tried to get my bearings. Two men shot past me and jumped overboard without even pausing. The storm wasn't so bad we needed to abandon ship, was it?

I looked to my youngest brother and saw him lapping up the rain, like a wildcat clawing at raw meat. When someone near him tried to do the same, they scrapped with each other, fighting over the drops. I backed away, turning to search for my middle brother. I never found him. He was lost in the crowd surging toward the water, gone before I

4

could make sense of what I was witnessing.

Then I saw my parents, hand in hand, their backs against the railing, casually tipping themselves overboard. They smiled. I screamed.

What was happening? Had the world gone mad?

A note caught my ear, and I dropped my hands, my fear and worries fading away as the song took hold. It did seem like it would be better to be in the water, embraced by the waves instead of pelted by rain. It sounded delicious. I needed to drink it. I needed to fill my stomach, my heart, my lungs with it.

With that sole desire pulsing through me, I walked toward the metal rails. It would be a pleasure to drink myself full until every last piece of me was sated. I was barely aware of hoisting myself over the side, barely aware of anything, until the hard smack of water on my face brought me back to my senses.

I was going to die.

No! I thought as I fought to get back to the surface. *I'm not ready! I want to live!* Nineteen years was not enough. There were still so many foods to taste and places to visit. A husband, I hoped, and a family. All of it, everything, gone in a split second.

Really?

I didn't have time to doubt the reality of the voice I was hearing. *Yes!*

What would you give to stay alive?

Anything!

In an instant, I was dragged out of the fray. It was as if an arm was looped around my waist, pulling with precision as I shot past body after body until I was free of them. I soon found myself lying on my back, staring up at three inhumanly lovely girls.

For a moment, all my horror and confusion disappeared. There was no storm, no family, no fear. All that ever had been or ever would be were these beautiful, perfect faces. I squinted, studying them, making the only guess that seemed possible.

"Are you angels?" I asked. "Am I dead?"

The closest girl, who had eyes as green as the emeralds in Mama's earrings and brilliant red hair that billowed around her face, bent down. "You're very much alive," she promised, her voice tinted with a British accent.

I gaped at her. If I was still alive, wouldn't I be feeling the scratch of salt down my throat? Wouldn't my eyes be burning from the water? Wouldn't I still be feeling the sting on my face from where I fell? Yet I felt perfect, complete. I was either dreaming or dead. I had to be.

In the distance, I could hear screams. I lifted my head, and just over the waves I spotted the tail of our ship as it bobbed surreally out of the water.

I took several ragged breaths, too confused to grasp

how I was still breathing, all the while listening to others drown around me.

"What do you remember?" she asked.

I shook my head. "The carpet." I searched my memories, already feeling them becoming distant and blurry. "And my mother's hair," I said, my voice cracking. "Then I was in the water."

"Did you ask to live?"

"I did," I sputtered, wondering if she could read my mind or if everyone else had thought it, too. "Who are you?"

"I'm Marilyn," she replied sweetly. "This is Aisling." She pointed to a blond girl who gave me a small, warm smile. "And that is Nombeko." Nombeko was as dark as the night sky and appeared to have nearly no hair at all. "We're singers. Sirens. Servants to the Ocean," Marilyn explained. "We help Her. We . . . feed Her."

I squinted. "What would the ocean eat?"

Marilyn glanced in the direction of the sinking ship, and I followed her gaze. Almost all the voices were quiet now.

Oh.

"It is our duty, and soon it could be yours as well. If you give your time to Her, She will give you life. From this day forward, for the next hundred years, you won't get sick or hurt, and you won't grow a day older. When your time is up, you'll get your voice back, your freedom back. You'll get to live."

"I'm sorry," I stammered. "I don't understand."

The others smiled behind her, but their eyes looked sad. "No. It would be impossible to understand now," Marilyn said. She ran her hand over my dripping hair, already treating me as if I was one of her own. "I assure you, none of us did. But you will."

Carefully, I raised myself until I was fully upright, shocked to see that I was standing on water. There were still a few people afloat in the distance, struggling in the current as if they thought they might be able to save themselves.

"My mother is there," I pleaded. Nombeko sighed, her eyes wistful.

Marilyn wrapped her arm around me, looking toward the wreckage. She whispered in my ear. "You have two choices: you may remain with us or you may join your mother. *Join* her. Not save her."

I stayed silent, thinking. Was she telling me the truth? Could I choose to die?

"You said you'd give anything to live," she reminded me. "Please mean it."

I saw the hope in her eyes. She didn't want me to go. Perhaps she'd seen enough death for one day.

I nodded. I'd stay.

She pulled me close and breathed into my ear. "Welcome to the sisterhood of sirens."

I was whipped underwater, something cold forced into my veins. And, though it frightened me, it hardly hurt at all.

80
YEARS
LATER

2

"Why?" she asked, her face bloated from drowning.

I held up my hands, warning her not to come any closer, trying to tell her without words that I was deadly. But it was clear she wasn't afraid. She was looking for revenge. And she would get it any way she could.

"Why?" she demanded again. Seaweed was wrapped around her leg, making a flat, wet sound as it dragged across the floor behind her.

The words were out of my mouth before I could stop myself. "I had to."

She didn't wince at my voice, just kept advancing. This was it. I would finally have to pay for what I had done.

"I had three children."

I backed away, looking for an escape. "I didn't know! I swear, I didn't know anything!"

Finally, she stopped, just inches from me. I waited for her to beat me or strangle me, to find a way to avenge the life taken from her far too soon. But she merely stood there, her head cocked sideways as she took me in, eyes bulging and skin tinted blue.

Then she lunged.

I awoke with a gasp, swinging my arm at the empty air in front of me before I understood.

A dream. It was only a dream. I placed a hand on my chest, hoping to slow my heart. Instead of finding skin, my fingers pressed into the back of my scrapbook. I picked it up, looking at the carefully constructed pages filled with clipped news articles. Served me right for working on it before sleeping.

I had just finished my page on Kerry Straus before falling asleep. She was one of the last people I needed to find from our most recent sinking. Two more to go, then I'd have information on every one of those lost souls. The *Arcatia* might be my first complete ship.

Looking down at Kerry's page, I took in the bright eyes from the photo on her memorial website, a shabby thing no doubt created by her widower husband between trying to serve up something more creative than spaghetti for his three motherless children and the endless routine of his day job. Kerry had a look of promise to her, an air of expectation hanging around her like a glow.

I took that from her. I stole it and fed it to the Ocean.

"At least you had a family," I told her photo. "At least there was someone to cry for you when you were gone." I wished I could explain to her how a full life cut short was better than an empty life that dragged on. I closed the book and set it in my trunk with the others, one for each shipwreck. There were only a handful of people who could possibly understand how I felt, and I wasn't always sure that they did.

With a heavy sigh, I made my way to the living room, where Elizabeth's and Miaka's voices were louder than I was comfortable with.

"Kahlen!" Elizabeth greeted. I tried to be inconspicuous as I checked to make sure all the windows were closed. They knew how important it was that no one could hear us, but they were never as cautious as I would have liked. "Miaka's just come up with another idea for her future."

I shifted my focus to Miaka. Tiny and dark in every way except for her spirit, she'd won me over in the first minutes I knew her.

"Do tell," I replied as I settled into the corner chair.

Miaka grinned widely at me. "I was thinking about buying a gallery."

15

"Really?" My eyebrows raised in surprise. "So owning instead of creating, huh?"

"I don't think you could ever actually stop painting," Elizabeth said thoughtfully.

I nodded. "You're too talented."

Miaka had been selling her art online for years. Even now, mid-conversation, she was tapping away on her phone, and I felt certain another big sale was in the works. The fact that any of us owned a phone was almost ridiculous— as if we had anyone to call—but she liked staying plugged in to the world.

"Being in charge of something seems like fun, you know?"

"I do," I said. "Ownership sounds incredibly appealing."

"Exactly!" Miaka typed and spoke at the same time. "Responsibility, individuality. It's all missing now, so maybe I can make up for it later."

I was about to say that we had plenty of responsibilities, but Elizabeth spoke up first.

"I had a new idea, too," she trilled.

"Tell us." Miaka set down her phone and climbed onto her as if they were puppies.

"I've decided I really like singing. I think I'd like to use it in a different way."

"You'd be a fantastic lead singer in a band."

Elizabeth sat up straight, nearly knocking Miaka to the floor. "That's exactly what I thought!"

I watched them, marveling at the fact that three such different people, born to different places and times and customs, could balance one another out so well. Even Aisling, when she chose to leave her self-imposed solitude and stay with us for a while, fit like a puzzle piece.

"What about you, Kahlen?"

"Huh?"

Miaka propped herself up. "Any new big dreams?"

We'd played this game hundreds of times over the years as a means of keeping our spirits up. I'd considered being a doctor so I could make amends for all the lives I'd taken. A dancer, so I could practice controlling my body in every capacity. A writer, so I could find a way to use my voice whether I spoke or not. An astronaut, in case I needed to put extra space between the Ocean and me. I had just about exhausted every possibility.

But deep down I knew there was only one thing I really wanted, something that was almost too painful to think about now.

I eyed the large history book that rested by my favorite chair—the book I'd meant to take back into my room last night—making sure the bridal magazine inside was still hidden from sight.

I smiled and shrugged. "Same old, same old."

I swallowed as I set foot onto campus. As much as I longed for a life as typical and pleasant as anyone else's, I never let myself get comfortable. Humans—and the constant need to keep silent for their protection—made me nervous. But even now, I could hear Elizabeth's voice in my head. "We don't need to stay inside all the time. I'm not living that way," she had vowed, maybe two weeks into her new life with us. And she had stayed true to her word, not only getting out herself, but making sure that the rest of us also had as much of a normal life as possible. Venturing out was half appeasement for her, half indulgence for myself.

Our current home was right near a university, which was perfect for me. It meant slews of people wandering around on open lawns and mingling at picnic tables. I didn't feel the need to go to concerts or clubs or parties like Elizabeth and Miaka. I was content merely to be among the humans, to watch them. Sure, maybe my sense of style was a little different, as I found myself forever drawn to the cut and lines of fifties skirts and dresses, but if I sat under a tree with a book, I could pretend to be one of them for hours.

I watched people pass, pleased we were in a town so friendly that some people waved to me for no reason at all. If I could have said hello to them—just one tiny, harmless word—the illusion would have been perfect.

". . . if she doesn't want to. I mean, why doesn't she just say something?" one girl asked the crowd of friends surrounding her. I imagined her a queen bee, the others hapless drones.

"You're totally right. She should have told you she didn't want to go instead of telling everyone else."

The queen flipped her hair. "Well, I'm done with her. I'm not playing those games."

I squinted after her, positive she was playing a completely different game, one she would certainly win.

"I'm telling you, man, we could design it." A short-haired boy waved his hands enthusiastically at his friend.

"I don't know." This boy, slightly overweight and scratching a patch of skin on his neck, was walking fast. He might have been trying to outwalk his friend, but his counterpart was so light on his feet, so motivated, that he probably could have kept up with a rocket.

"Just a tiny investment, man. We could be the next big thing. In ten years, people could be talking about those two nerds from Florida who changed their worlds!"

I suppressed a smile.

When the crowds dispersed in the afternoon, I made my way to the library. Since moving to Miami, I'd gone there once or twice a week. I didn't like to do my scrapbook research at the house. I'd made that mistake before, and Elizabeth had mocked me mercilessly for being morbid.

"Why don't you just go hunt for their corpses?" she'd said. "Or ask the Ocean to tell you their final thoughts. You want to know that, too?"

I understood her disgust. She saw my scrapbooks as an unhealthy obsession with the people we'd murdered. What I wished she understood was the way those people haunted me, the way the screams stayed with me long after the ships sank. Knowing that Melinda Bernard had a vast collection of dolls and that Jordan Cammers was in his first year of medical school eased my pain. Like somehow knowing more about their lives than their deaths made things better for them.

My goal today was Warner Thomas, the second-to-last person on the passenger list of the *Arcatia*. Warner turned out to be a relatively easy subject. There were tons of people with the same name, but once I'd found all the social networking profiles with posts that stopped abruptly six months ago, I knew he was the right one. Warner was a string bean of a man who looked too shy to talk to people in person. He was listed as single everywhere, and I felt bad for thinking that made perfect sense.

The last entry on his blog was heartbreaking.

Sorry this is short, but I'm updating from my phone.

Look at this sunset!

Just below that line, the sun melted into nothing on the back of the Ocean.

> So much beauty in the world! Can't help but think good
> things are on the way!

I nearly laughed. His expression in every picture made me think he'd never exclaimed anything in his life. But I couldn't help wondering whether something had happened just before that fateful trip. Did he have a reason to think the direction of his life was changing? Or was it one of those lies we told from the safety of our rooms when no one could see how false it was?

I printed out the best-looking photo of him, a joke he'd posted, and some information about his siblings. The scrapbooks weren't things I liked to carry in public, so I placed my papers neatly in my bag to take home.

Sorry, Warner. I swear, it wasn't me you died for.

With that complete, I was able to turn my mind to something a little more fun. I had learned over the years to balance out each devastating piece of my scrapbook with something joyful. Last night, it was looking at dresses before pasting in the last of Kerry's pictures. Today, it was cakes. I found the culinary section and hoisted a stack of books to an empty space on the third floor. I pored over recipes, fondant work, construction. I built imaginary wedding cakes, one at a time, indulging in the most consistent of my daydreams. The first, a classic vanilla and buttercream with pale-blue frosting and little white poppies. Three tiers. Very lovely. The next was five tiers, square, with black ribbon and costume jewelry brooches aligned vertically on the front. A bit more appropriate for an evening wedding.

Maybe this would be my next big dream. Maybe I could become a baker and make someone else's day special on the off chance I never got one myself.

"You having a party?"

I looked up to see a scruffy, blond-haired boy pushing a cart full of books. He had a flimsy name tag I couldn't read and was wearing the standard college boy uniform of khaki pants and a button-up shirt with his sleeves cuffed around his elbows. No one tried anymore.

I held back my sigh. It was unavoidable, this part of the sentence. We were meant to draw people in, and men were particularly susceptible.

I looked down again without answering, hoping he'd take the hint. I hadn't chosen to sit at the back of the top floor because I felt like socializing.

"You look stressed. You could probably use a party."

I couldn't suppress my smirk. He had no idea. Unfortunately, he took that little smile as an invitation to continue.

He ran his hand through his hair, the modern-day equivalent of "Good day, miss," and pointed at the books. "My mom says the secret to making good baked stuff is to use a warm bowl. Not that I'd know. I can hardly make cereal without burning it."

His grin suggested that this was only too true, and I was slightly charmed as he bashfully tucked a hand into his pocket.

It was a pity, really. I knew he meant no harm, and I didn't want to hurt his feelings. But I was about to resort to the rudest move I had and simply walk away when he pulled that same hand back out and extended it to me.

"I'm Akinli, by the way," he said, waiting for me to respond. I gawked at him, not used to people pressing past my silence. "I know it's weird." He'd misread my confusion. "Family name. Kind of. It was a last name on my mom's side of the family."

He kept his palm outstretched, waiting. Typically my response would be to flee. But Elizabeth and Miaka managed to interact with others. For goodness' sakes, Elizabeth cycled through lovers regularly without ever saying a word. And there was something about this boy that seemed . . . different. Maybe it was how his lips lifted into a smile without him seeming to even think about it, or the way his voice rolled warmly out of him like clouds, but I felt certain snubbing him would end up hurting my feelings more than his, and that I'd regret it.

Cautiously, as if I might break us both, I took his hand, hoping he wouldn't notice how cool my skin was.

"And you are?" he prompted.

I sighed, sure this would end the conversation despite

my kindest intentions. I signed my name, and his eyes widened.

"Oh, wow. So have you been reading my lips this whole time?"

I shook my head.

"You can hear?"

I nodded.

"But you can't speak. . . . Umm, okay." He started patting at his pockets as I tried to fight the dread creeping down my spine. We didn't have many rules, but the ones we did have were absolute. Stay silent in the presence of others, until it was time to sing. When the time came to sing, do it without hesitation. When we weren't singing, do nothing to expose our secret. Walking down the street was one thing, and so was sitting under a tree. But this? An attempt at an actual conversation? It landed me in a very dangerous realm.

"Here we go," he announced, pulling out a pen. "I don't have any paper, so you'll have to write on my hand."

I stared at his skin, debating. Which name should I use? The one on the driver's license Miaka bought me online? The one I'd used to rent our current beach house? The one I'd used in the last town we'd stayed in? I had a hundred names to choose from.

Perhaps foolishly, I chose to tell him the truth.

"Kahlen?" he read off his skin.

I nodded, surprised by how freeing it felt to have one human on the planet know my birth name.

"That's pretty. Nice to meet you."

I gave him a thin smile, still uncomfortable. I didn't know how to do small talk.

"That's really cool that you're going to a traditional school even though you use sign language. I thought I was brave just getting out of state." He laughed at himself.

Even with how uneasy I was feeling, I admired his effort to keep the conversation going. It was more than most people would do in his situation. He pointed at the books again. "So, uh, if you ever have that party and need some help with your cake, I swear I could get my act together long enough not to ruin everything."

I raised one eyebrow at him.

"I'm serious!" He laughed like I'd told a joke. "Anyway, good luck with that. See you around."

He waved sheepishly, then continued pushing his cart down the aisle. I watched him go. I knew I'd remember his hair, a mess that looked windswept even in stillness, and the kindness in his eyes. And I'd hate myself for holding on to those details if he ever crossed my path on one of those dark days, like the days when Kerry or Warner had encountered me.

Still, I was grateful. I couldn't recall the last time I'd felt so human.

3

"What do you want to do tonight?" Elizabeth asked, flopping onto the couch. Outside the window behind her, the sky was fading from blue to pink to orange, and I mentally ticked off one more day of the thousands I had left. "I actually don't feel like going to a club."

"Whoa, whoa, whoa!" I threw my arms up. "Are you sick?" I teased.

"Ha-ha," she retorted. "I'm just in the mood for something different."

Miaka looked up from our shared laptop. "Where is it daytime? We could go to a museum."

Elizabeth shook her head. "I will never understand how

you are so into such quiet buildings. As if we aren't silent enough."

"Pssh!" I gave her a pointed look. "You, silent?"

Elizabeth stuck out her tongue at me and hopped over to Miaka. "What are you looking at?"

"Skydiving."

"Oh, wow! Now that's more like it!"

"Don't get any big ideas. For now I'm just researching. I've been wondering what would happen with our adrenaline levels if we did something like this," Miaka said, taking notes on a pad beside the computer. Like, if we'd get an above-average spike."

I chuckled. "Miaka, is this an adventure or a science experiment?"

"A little bit of both. I've read that adrenaline rushes can alter your perception, making things look blurry or causing a moment to look frozen. I think it'd be interesting to do something like this, see what I see, then try to capture it in art."

I smiled. "I admit, it's creative. But there has to be a better way to get a rush than jumping out of a plane."

"Even if things went wrong, we'd survive, right?" Miaka questioned, and they both turned to me as if I was an authority figure on the topic.

"I think so. Either way, you can count me out for that particular adventure."

"Scared?" Elizabeth made wiggly ghost fingers at me.

"No," I protested. "Simply not interested."

"She's afraid she'll get in trouble," Miaka guessed. "That the Ocean wouldn't like it."

"As if She would ever get upset with you," Elizabeth said, a tinge of bitterness in her voice. "She adores you."

"She cares for all of us." I tucked my hands in my lap.

"Then She wouldn't mind if you went skydiving."

"What if you're terrified and start screaming?" I proposed. "What would that do?"

Elizabeth, who was preparing to pounce on my worry, backed down. "Fair point."

"I have twenty years to go," I said quietly. "If I mess up now, it'd make the last eighty years a waste. You know the stories about sirens who went wrong as well as I do. Miaka, you *saw* what happened to Ifama."

Miaka shuddered. The Ocean had saved Ifama as she was drowning off the coast of South Africa in the fifties, and she had agreed to serve in exchange for being able to live. For the short season she was with us, she kept her distance, staying alone in her room, appearing to be in prayer most of the time. Later we wondered if her coldness was part of a plan to remain unattached to us. When she had to sing for the first time, she stood on the water, chin in the air, and refused. The Ocean pulled her under so fast, it was as if she'd never been there at all.

It was a warning to us all. We must sing, and we must keep the secret. It was a short list of commandments.

"And what about Catarina?" I continued. "Or Beth? Or Molly? What about the slew of girls in our position who failed?"

These girls' stories were the cautionary tales that were passed down from one siren to the next. Beth had used her voice to make three girls who had teased her jump into a well. This was in the late 1600s when the idea of witches wasn't that far-fetched. She'd put an entire town in an uproar, and the Ocean had silenced her to keep our secret. Catarina was another who had refused to sing and was taken. The strange thing about her was that she'd already been a siren for thirty years at that point. I nearly made myself crazy wondering about what could have made her give up on the promise of freedom that far in.

Molly's story was different—and more disturbing. Her life as a siren had brought on some kind of mental breakdown. Four years in, she'd murdered a household of people in the night, including an infant, in an outburst she hadn't realized she'd had until she was standing over an elderly woman who was facedown in a bathtub. From what I had heard, the Ocean tried to soothe her, but when she had a similar episode a few months later, the Ocean took her life. Molly was proof that there was grace when the Ocean knew your intentions, but she also showed that there was only so much room for that mercy.

These were the stories we carried, the guardrails that kept us in line. Forsaking the rules meant forsaking your life.

Exposing our secret would mean being taken away, maybe experimented on. When they couldn't destroy us, and if we couldn't escape, that could be a literal eternity of silent imprisonment. And if anyone guessed that the Ocean was purposefully consuming some of the people She also helped sustain, it wouldn't take the humans very long to figure out how to get their water without ever touching Her. If no one went into the water . . . how would we all live?

Obedience was imperative.

"I worry about you two," I confessed, crossing the room to hug them. "Honestly, I'm jealous sometimes of how well you've both . . . assimilated. But I wonder how much longer you can do that without making a mistake."

"You don't have to worry," Miaka assured me. "This is what sirens have done throughout history, and we just happen to be the best at it so far. Even Aisling lives on the outskirts of a town. Human contact helps to keep us sane. You don't have to seclude yourself to make it through this life."

I nodded. "I know. But I don't want to push my limits, or the Ocean's."

Elizabeth didn't need to say anything. I could hear her

judgment without words.

"Why don't we go see Aisling?" Miaka suggested. "We've never really asked her about how she copes."

"Because she's never here," Elizabeth replied, irritation in her voice.

We hadn't seen our fourth sister since the last time we sang, and it had been well over two years since she'd lived with us.

"That might be a good idea. Just a short trip," I added, mainly for Elizabeth, who had never really warmed to Aisling. She was too reclusive for Elizabeth's taste.

Elizabeth nodded. "Sure. Nothing else going on anyway."

We headed out the back door where a small wooden staircase led down to a floating dock. A handful of the other houses had Jet Skis or personal paddleboats secured to theirs, but ours was empty. The sun was low enough that no one would see as we slipped into the water.

Her currents stirred in greeting, and an almost tickling feeling wrapped around my body as we sank in. I relaxed in the warmth of Her embrace, already calmer.

Can you tell Aisling we're coming? I asked.

Of course.

Wheee! Elizabeth sang as we dived deep into the water and set off. The speed stripped away her flimsy clothes, and she spread out her arms, hair dancing behind her, as she waited for her siren's dress.

31

When we moved like this, every earthly thing we wore fell away. The Ocean opened Her veins, releasing thousands of particles of salt that affixed themselves to our bodies, creating long, delicate flowing gowns. They were gorgeous, coming out in every shade of Her—the purple of a patch of coral that human eyes had never passed, the green of kelp growing toward the light, the gold of burning sand at sunrise—and were never exactly the same thing twice. It was almost painful to watch them fall apart, one grain at a time, rarely lasting more than a few days after we left Her.

You seem sad. Her words came only to my ears.

I've been having more nightmares, I admitted.

You don't have to sleep. You'll be fine without it, you know that.

I smiled. *I do. But I like sleep. It's soothing. I'd just like to have it without the dreams is all.*

She couldn't take away my dreams, but She always comforted me as best She could. Sometimes She took me to islands or showed me the prettiest parts of Herself, so easily hidden from humans. Sometimes She knew that caring for me meant letting me be apart from Her. I never wanted to be away from Her for too long, though. She was the only mother I had, now.

Part mother, part warden, part employer . . . it was a hard relationship to explain.

Aisling swam out to greet us, her own dress partially formed and floating in strands around her.

What a surprise! she greeted, squeezing Miaka's hand. *Follow me.*

We trailed behind her, skirting around the plates of land as they pushed themselves above the water into continents. Our sense of geography was a bit specialized, knowing that some places were surrounded by rocks, others by sand, others by sheer cliffs. There were other things we knew by heart as well, like the places we'd found each other or the locations of ships we'd taken down, a peculiar knowledge of unmapped ghost towns on the Ocean's floor.

We tailed Aisling as she went to a slightly uneven coast, pulling herself upright as soon as the water was shallow enough.

"Don't worry," she said, taking in our nerves when she brazenly exited onto land. "We're all alone out here."

"I thought you lived near a town," Elizabeth said, hopping across the rounded rocks as we crossed the shore.

Aisling shrugged. "Distance is relative." She led us to an aging cottage just beyond the tree line. It was picturesque, settled underneath some heavy branches, and I imagined those limbs cooling the space in the summer and protecting her from snow in the winter. In front was a small garden bursting with flowers and berries, and the way everything flourished made me feel that, while the rest of us were connected solely to water, Aisling had drawn strength from all the elements.

"This place is so small!" Miaka commented on entering. It was one room, barely the size of the living room in our beach house. There wasn't much in the way of furniture, just a small bed and a bench along one side of a table.

"I think it's cozy," Aisling remarked, placing a kettle on an ancient stove. "It's nice of you to come. I picked some fresh berries today and was making a pie. Give me forty-five minutes, and we should have a magnificent dessert!"

"Expecting company?" Elizabeth asked. "Or just incredibly bored?"

We didn't have many reasons to cook. We didn't need food, and Elizabeth especially could go for months before the craving for a particular taste hit her.

Aisling smiled as she finished lining the bottom of her pan. "Yes, the king should be dropping by any moment."

"Ah, the king likes pie?" Miaka joked back.

"Everyone likes pie!" she teased, and sighed. "I was a little bored today, to tell you the truth. So I'm very happy for your visit."

I stood beside Aisling as she poured the filling. "You know, you can always come stay with us."

"Oh, I like the quiet."

"You just told us you were bored," Miaka said, her artist's eyes exploring the room.

"One day out of a hundred," Aisling said, dismissing us. "But I know I should spend more time with you all these days. I'll try."

"You okay?" I asked. "You seem keyed up."

Aisling plastered a smile on her face. "I'm great. Just happy to see you all. What's the occasion?"

"Can you please tell Kahlen to calm down?" Elizabeth asked, sitting on the lone bed looking as if she owned the place. "She's moping again. Dabbling with the scrapbooks, afraid her world will end if so much as the shadow of a human crosses her path."

Aisling and I shared a look, and she grinned. "What's really going on?"

"Nothing," I swore. "We're just comparing coping mechanisms. I feel safer when we're more anonymous. The fewer people we interact with, the better."

"And yet you insist on living in big cities," Elizabeth grumbled.

I rolled my eyes. "So we blend in easier."

Miaka walked over, placing a tiny hand on Aisling's shoulder. "I think what Elizabeth means is, since you're the oldest, you might have some wisdom to pass on."

Aisling took off her apron, and we all sat together, crowding on the bench and the bed. "Well, let's be honest. The Ocean doesn't need more than one of us at a time. She could do Her work with a single siren. But She makes sure there are at least two at all times so we won't be alone."

"And we have the Ocean," I added.

"Which is weird. She's hard to understand." Elizabeth toyed with the salty sparkles of her dress.

"She's not a person," I pointed out. "Of course She's hard to understand."

"Back to the matter at hand: Aisling, don't you think it's possible to interact with humans without consequence?" Elizabeth pressed.

Aisling smiled to herself, her eyes fixed on a blank space in the air. "Definitely. In fact, I think seeing lives that actually change and have seasons has added to my life even though I can't change myself. It's about knowing your limits, I think." She drew her gaze back to Elizabeth. "It seems to me Kahlen knows hers, so maybe we should respect them."

"Well, it seems to *me* like she's miserable and would be much happier if she stepped out into the real world every once in a while." Elizabeth grinned, a snippy smile that wasn't asking for a fight but let us all know she still thought she knew best.

"Along the same lines," Miaka said, straightening up. "Skydiving. Would you do it, Aisling?"

Aisling laughed nervously. "I don't like heights, so probably not."

Miaka nodded. "I admit, the falling would be weird.

But I want to see the world from above."

"You've seen wars, watched countries disappear and re-form. You have experienced more seasons of fashion than most people can remember. We walked the Great Wall, you rode an elephant. . . . For goodness' sakes, Elizabeth took us to see the Beatles!" I reminded her. "Do you really need anything more?"

Miaka beamed. "I want to see everything."

We passed the rest of our visit talking about paintings Miaka had made, books I had read, movies Elizabeth had seen. Aisling really meant it when she said she enjoyed watching the lives around her, and she told us how the best baker in town was finally closing her shop and how there was a boom recently in people hired as dog walkers. It was all a bunch of nothing to me, but everything to these strangers who were living it.

"I wish I had a talent like you, Miaka," Aisling lamented after hearing her theories on adrenaline and art. "I feel like I don't have anything to say. Right now, my life is very still."

"You really are welcome to stay with us," I offered again.

She leaned into me, our heads touching. "I know. It just seems like life is very fast these days. I won't have this quiet much longer. I think I'll miss it."

"Fast?" I questioned. "What are you doing that makes

the years pass any faster than a crawl?"

"I agree with Aisling, actually. Everything is fast," Elizabeth commented. "There's not enough time to do everything I want. But I love it!"

After a few hours, Elizabeth got antsy, so I politely said it was time to get home. Aisling held me back as Miaka and Elizabeth headed toward the water.

"I can't tell you what to do, but I know how much our work haunts you. If the way you've been living for eighty years isn't making you feel better, maybe it's time to try something different."

"But what if I mess up?"

She squeezed my hand. "You're too good to mess up. And if you did, you are the most likely to be pardoned. She loves you. You know that."

I nodded. "Thank you."

"Any time. I'll come visit soon."

She trotted back into the house, and I considered her advice while I watched her through the window as she began the process of making another pie.

I smiled to myself. Aisling had nothing to lose or gain by telling me to change my habits, which made me trust her. So I held my feelings and worries and questions in my heart, considering if maybe there was a way for me to make my final stretch of this life any easier.

4

I spent the majority of the following evening letting Miaka curl my hair. I didn't understand the way my sisters lived their lives, and I wasn't sure it was wise, but I'd never really tried to walk a mile in their heels. Tonight, I would.

"What do you think of this one?" Elizabeth held up another dress. Basically, everything she showed me looked like a short tube of fabric, only in a different color.

"I don't know. It's not quite my style."

She cocked her head. "That's kind of the point. You can't go to a club looking like a fifties housewife."

I wrinkled my nose. "It's a bit . . . revealing, don't you think?"

Miaka chuckled as Elizabeth widened her eyes in frustration. "Yes. Very. Just put it on, okay?" She tossed the dress at me, and it landed in a heap on my lap. "I'm going to get dressed," she called, rushing out of the room.

I held back a sigh. After all, I was trying to be enthusiastic. Maybe tonight would usher in a new beginning in my life.

"We should do your hair like this more often," Miaka said, prompting me to turn to the mirror.

I gasped. "It's so full!"

"A few hours of dancing will deflate it."

I leaned in, studying my face. I'd gotten used to the natural beauty that came with being a siren. Miaka's artful strokes of eyeliner and lipstick magnified it by ten. I could see why boys practically formed a line for Elizabeth's attention.

"Thanks. You did great."

She shrugged. "Any time." Then she leaned in toward the mirror to do her own face.

"So what do we do when we get there?" I asked. "I don't know how to act in a crowded room."

"There's not a step-by-step program on how to go out and have a good time, Kahlen. We'll probably get a drink and scope out the crowd. Elizabeth will be looking for someone for sure, but you and I can just dance with each other."

"I gave up understanding how young people dance

about thirty years ago. The Electric Slide was the final nail in the coffin for me."

"But dancing's so fun!"

I shook my head. "No. The jitterbug was fun. But actually having rhythm and holding your partner's hand isn't popular anymore."

Miaka pulled the mascara wand away from her face, trying not to poke her eye while she laughed. "I swear, if you try to whip out the jitterbug tonight, Elizabeth will kill you."

"Good luck with that," I muttered. "Anyway, all I'm trying to say is that I might not be on the dance floor too much."

Miaka's gaze met mine in the mirror. "I'm happy you're going somewhere that isn't a library or a park, but I'm not sure it's really taking a chance if you just sit there."

"Ta-da!" Elizabeth sang, bursting into the room. Her dress was black and short, and she was wearing the shoes she referred to as "stripper heels." "So?"

I smiled. "What can I say? You could stop traffic."

She beamed, fluffing her hair with a hand. "I found this," she said, bringing something over to me.

It was another short dress, but it had a thin layer of tulle from the waist down. And, yes, it was covered with sequins, but it was closer to my style than anything else she'd shown me.

I smiled. "Thanks. This is the one."

Elizabeth threw her arms around me. "I'm so happy you're coming! The only thing better than being the two prettiest girls in the room is being the three prettiest!"

The bouncer was under Elizabeth's spell from the moment he saw her coming, and I had the feeling that even if our fake IDs hadn't said we were twenty-one, we would have been walking through the door without Xs on our hands anyway.

I cringed away from the blaring bass, already second-guessing my choice to come. Perhaps sensing that, Miaka looped her arm through mine, pulling me to the bar. She typed out our drink orders on her phone, and we carried our glasses carefully through the crowd.

This is supposed to be fun, I told myself. *Just try. This makes life better for your sisters. It could do the same for you.*

"How can you think in here?" I whispered into Elizabeth's ear.

She placed her lips next to my ear and answered, "The point is *not* to think."

"Relax," Miaka signed. "This is no different than walking down a crowded street."

And I tried; I did. I had two drinks, hoping to take the edge off my nerves. I danced with Miaka, which was fun until we garnered so many admirers intent on pressing themselves against us that it lost all its charm. I even tried just focusing on the music, something that should come naturally to a siren, but the way it blasted through the speakers turned it all into noise.

I watched the strange way some people moved toward Elizabeth as if she were a magnet on the dance floor. It was no surprise that she could hook someone without a word. We truly were the most beautiful girls in the room, and when Elizabeth turned her full attention on a boy, he was helpless. First, she picked one who was eventually pulled away by his friends to hit up another bar. Even without her song, he put up a little fight to stay until they wrestled him out the door. Her second choice had more to drink than she realized, and he passed out at their table.

But after two miserable hours, she came walking by again, an obviously drunk guy on her arm. "Don't wait up," she signed, disappearing with him out the door.

I turned to Miaka, eyes pleading. She grinned and nodded, and with that we headed home.

"You tried," she signed as we walked down the sidewalk. "I thought we'd lose you before we got in."

"You nearly did," I confessed. "Now I know for sure: the club scene is not for me."

"Do you think you'd come to a house party or something? We get invited to lots if we walk across campus at the right time."

My signs were hesitant. "Baby steps."

Clicking down the row of clubs in our heels garnered whistles from some and applause from others. I subconsciously placed a hand over my cleavage, though it really did no good. Miaka grinned to herself, standing a little taller as she walked, and I wondered if part of the charm of this lifestyle for my sisters was simply being seen. Most days, we kept to ourselves, and during our singing, the picture we painted was nothing but a lie. At least, like this, someone saw us live. Though, for me, it felt less like being seen and more like being viewed.

When we got to the house, I didn't bother to take off Elizabeth's dress before running out the back door and hopping into the water.

Kahlen! The Ocean surged around me, welcoming and calm.

You wouldn't believe the night I just had.

Tell me everything. I drew up a mental picture of Her resting Her chin on Her hand, hanging on my every word.

Miaka and Elizabeth like going to clubs, these places where people drink and dance. They've been telling me to get out more, so I finally went with them.

I can't imagine you doing that.

Neither could I. Which is why I was uncomfortable the entire time. I'm so happy to be back here. You're nice and quiet.

Her waters stirred in something close to laughter. *We*

don't have to talk at all if you don't want to. I'm happy just to hold you.

I sank down, resting on the sandy Ocean floor, legs crossed and arms behind my head. I watched the trails of boats crisscrossing and fading along the surface above me. Fish swam by in schools, not spooked by the girl on the ground.

So, about six months? I asked, my stomach twisting.

Yes, barring some natural disaster or man-made sinking. I can't predict those things.

I know.

Don't start worrying about that yet. I can tell you're still hurting from the last time. She wrapped me in sympathy.

I lifted my arms as if I was stroking Her, though of course my tiny body was unable to truly embrace Hers. *I feel like I never have enough time to get over a singing before the next one comes. I have nightmares, and I'm a nervous wreck during the weeks leading up to it.* My chest felt hollow with misery. *I'm afraid I'll always remember how it feels.*

You won't. In all My years, I've never had a freed siren come back to Me demanding that I fix her memories.

Do You hear from them at all?

Not intentionally. I feel people when they're in Me. It's how I find new girls. It's how I listen for anyone who might suspect the true nature of My needs. Sometimes a former siren will go for a swim or stick her legs off a dock. I can get a peek at their lives, and no one has remembered Me yet.

I'll remember You, I promised.

I could feel Her embracing me. *For all eternity, I'll never forget you. I love you.*

And I love You.

You can rest here tonight, if you like. I'll make sure no one finds you.

Can I just stay down here forever? I don't want to worry about hurting people unintentionally. Or disappointing my sisters. Aisling has her cottage, so maybe I could build a little house down here out of driftwood.

She ran a current down my back gently. *Sleep. You'll feel differently in the morning. Your sisters would be lost without you. Trust Me, they think it all the time.*

Really?

Really.

Thank You.

Rest. You're safe.

5

I held the baby close to me, trying to get her to stop crying.

"Shh," I urged, hoping my voice would somehow comfort her instead of cause her more pain.

"It's okay," I whispered as she thrashed in my arms. The streams of tears from her eyes grew denser and faster, until water was pouring from her. Then her cries became gargles as water flooded from her mouth as well.

I shook in horror watching her drown from the inside out.

I jerked awake, forgetting I was underwater and feeling as if I were drowning as well. I screamed in spite of myself.

You're safe, Kahlen! You're safe!

I clutched my hands around my throat and chest, terrified until I understood who was speaking to me and that what She said was true.

I'm sorry. I had a nightmare.

I know.

I sighed. Of course She knew.

Go to your sisters. As much as I love having you with Me, you need to be on land. You need sunlight.

I nodded. *You're right. I'll visit again soon.*

I pushed myself toward the surface, trying to conceal how deeply I wanted to be free from Her watery hold now. It was hard to balance that with how desperately I had wanted to hide in Her only hours ago.

I climbed onto the floating dock just in time to see the sun break through the clouds. I stood there, trying to unknot my feelings. Fear, hope, worry, compassion . . . there was so much going on in my heart, I felt paralyzed. Aisling wanted me to get out of my routine. Elizabeth and Miaka wanted me to get out of my comfort zone. I sensed none of that could happen until I could get out of the mess I was inside.

I walked up the stairs and back into the house. Elizabeth was home, still clad in her little black dress, her shoes left sloppily by the door. She was laughing with Miaka, drinking a coffee she'd bought on the way home, buzzing from the night before.

They both turned to the sight of me walking through

the doorway, and Elizabeth's face immediately fell.

"Please don't tell me you got in the water in that dress!"

I looked down at the droplets pooling on the floor. "Umm, yeah, I did."

"It's dry-clean only!"

"Sorry. I'll replace it."

"What's wrong?" Miaka asked, seeing past everything else to my misery.

"Just more bad dreams," I confessed, peeling off the dress. I needed something softer, warmer. "I'm okay. I think I'm going to curl up with a book."

"We're here if you want to talk," Miaka offered.

"Thanks. I'll be fine."

I walked back to my room, not wanting to hear Elizabeth relive her latest conquest. Though I really had no desire to get back into water, I kind of wanted to wash the sea salt smell off my skin. As much as I could anyway.

"Why does she even bother sleeping?" I heard Elizabeth ask quietly. "You'd think by now she'd stop trying. We don't need it."

I paused, waiting to hear Miaka's response. "She must have a really wonderful dream often enough to make the bad ones worth it."

I closed the door all the way, hung Elizabeth's dress out my window, and let the spray of the shower cloud out everything else.

* * *

I flipped through my scrapbooks, searching. Finally, on a page for a sinking that was maybe twelve years old, I found the face of the baby in my dream. The Ocean assured me that I wouldn't remember any of this, so why did the faces linger with me now? Elizabeth would say it was because I insisted on documenting it all, but I knew that wasn't it. At least, not completely.

I'd made a rule for myself not to look at people's faces while the sinkings happened, but I failed more than I cared to admit. It was hard to ignore the people calling out for us to save them. Sometimes I'd see someone and then never find a public record of them. No obituary or blog or anything. I knew those faces as well as I knew the ones in my books.

Sometimes I wondered if I was broken, which worried me as much as any of our singings. If I could remember the tens of thousands of people I'd killed, how would I possibly survive my life after being a siren?

I looked down at the picture of the baby, a girl named Norah, and cried over the life she never got to live.

Even though I knew the next singing was still nearly six months away, I dreaded it like it was coming tomorrow. It felt as if my very soul was being chipped away at every time it happened. Eighty long years gone. Twenty more to go. And each day felt as if it were never-ending.

Monday morning, I got out of the house as fast as I could. I grabbed one of Miaka's many sketchbooks and shoved it into my bag along with some pencils. I'd dabbled in painting and drawing ever since Miaka came home with her first canvas, and while I would never be the artist she was, the idea of occupying my hands for a while sounded good.

I made my way to campus, taking the quietest roads I could find, and crossed onto the main area near the fountain and library just as people were making their way to class. Part of me felt bad for being so hard on Elizabeth and Miaka. They blended in at bars and clubs. I blended in at the library. Maybe their way of handling things didn't work for me, but that didn't mean it wasn't valid.

I settled under a tree and pulled out the sketch pad, thinking I'd draw some of the outfits I saw. I loved seeing how fashion changed over time, and though I preferred a more classic style, it was fun to see how a headband or the height of a shoe or the cut of a neckline would bring back something I'd come across twenty years before.

I'd seen this as a problem for my fair share of people, though. I'd watched some get stuck in the eighties, doing unthinkable things to their hair, or wearing bell-bottoms when it wasn't the best idea. Maybe staying in a favorite era was like a security blanket, something you could keep when everything else changed. I fanned out my circle skirt and figured that was true.

Then, unexpectedly, someone settled in next to me under the shade of my tree.

"Okay, so I was thinking you were a culinary student, but this has me considering art instead."

It was the boy from the library, Akinli.

"I'm undecided, personally. You're not judging me, are you?"

I smiled and shook my head. I liked that he just started speaking as if we were already in the middle of a conversation.

"Good. I've been considering a few things. Like finance sounds like a smart way to go, but I'm about as bad with money as I am at cooking."

I smiled, scribbling in the corner of my page. *But isn't that why people study? To get better?*

"That's a good argument, but I think you're overestimating my skills."

He grinned back at me, and I remembered how normal he'd made me feel the first time we'd met. Here, once again, he wasn't bothered by my silence. And I suddenly realized what made me feel so uncomfortable about Elizabeth's exploits. The people she attracted were drawn to the same thing everyone else was: our glowing skin, dreamy eyes, and air of secrecy. But this boy? He seemed to see more than that. He saw me not just as a mysterious beauty, but as a girl he wanted to know.

He didn't stare at me. He spoke to me.

"So did you make that epic cake this weekend or what?"

I shook my head. *I went to my first club,* I wrote, pleased with how normal that confession seemed.

"And?"

Not really my thing.

"Yeah, I was a designated driver on Friday, and I seriously can't stand the stench of bars. It's like there's an old cigarette smell clinging to the walls even though you can't smoke in them anymore." Akinli scrunched up his nose in disgust. "Plus, even though I like the guys on my hall, I don't like them enough to be okay with cleaning puke off two of them. I think my days as a chauffeur are officially over."

I made a face and shook my head. I understood that babysitter feeling a little too well.

"Any classes left today?"

Nope!

"See, I'm totally jealous. I thought afternoon classes would mean sleeping in, which was a brilliant plan on my part because I'm in a serious relationship with sleep."

Me too.

"Well, I think I'd let the relationship suffer a little if it meant I could do more in the afternoons. Look at you. You're free to sit in the sun and creepily draw pictures of people you don't even know. How great is that?"

I smirked. I often thought of myself as kind of creepy. This was the first time it sounded like a good thing.

It's the clothes! I argued, pointing to the pages.

"Uh-huh. Whatever you say. But don't mind me. I'm just jealous. I can't draw at all. The only thing I know how to make is a frog. I learned how in the first grade, and I never forgot. The key is starting with a football shape," he said, his voice full of mock expertise. "If you get that wrong, the whole thing goes downhill."

Can't cook. Can't draw. What can you do?

"Excellent question. Um . . . I can fish. Family thing, much like the terrible, terrible first name. I can text in complete sentences. Oh, yeah, it's a skill." He smiled, proud of his accomplishments. "And, thanks to my mom being a competitive dancer as a teen, I know how to do the Lindy hop and the jitterbug."

I sat bolt upright, and Akinli rolled his eyes.

"I swear, if you tell me you can jitterbug, I'm going to . . . I don't even know. Set something on fire. No one can dance like that."

I pursed my lips and dusted off my shoulder, a thing I'd seen Elizabeth do when she was bragging.

As if he was accepting a challenge, he shrugged off his backpack and stood, holding out a hand for me.

I took it and positioned myself in front of him as he

54

shook his head, grinning.

"All right, we'll take this slow. Five, six, seven, eight."

In unison, we rock stepped and triple stepped, falling into the rhythm in our head. After a minute, he got brave and swung me around, lining me up for those peppy kicks I loved so much.

People walked by, pointing and laughing, but it was one of those moments when I knew we weren't being mocked; we were being envied.

We stepped on each other's toes more than once, and after he accidentally knocked his head into my shoulder, he threw his hands up.

"Unbelievable," he said, almost as if he was complaining. "I can't wait to tell my mom this. She's gonna think I'm lying. All those years dancing in the kitchen thinking I was special, and then I run across a master."

We sat back down under the tree, and I started collecting my things. That was a pretty little moment, and I was almost afraid another minute in his presence would break it.

"So you didn't make that cake yet?"

I shook my head.

"Well, since you're swearing off clubs, and I'm swearing off driving for drunks, and there's really not an appropriate venue downtown to show off our dance skills, why don't we make it this weekend?"

I raised an eyebrow.

"Look, I know what I said about being a bad cook, but I think you could keep me from ruining it."

Now who's overestimating skills?

He laughed. "No, seriously, I think it'd be fun. If all else fails, I've got some Easy Mac in my room, so we'll at least have something to eat."

I shrugged, dubious but tempted. Elizabeth could regularly go to a stranger's apartment, be as intimate as two people could be, and live to tell the tale. So, maybe I could bake in a dorm kitchen without murdering someone?

"You seem nervous. You got a boyfriend?"

He said the last as if he was only belatedly realizing the obvious.

I wrote *NO* in big letters on the paper.

He chuckled again. "Okay." He took the pen from my hand, scribbling onto a sticky note. "Here's my number. If you decide you want to come over, text me."

I nodded and took his number, and his whole face lit up. He checked his phone.

"All right, now I'm running late." He pushed himself up to his feet. "Catch you later, Kahlen." He pointed at me. "See? I remembered."

I fought my smile, not wanting him to know how much the small gesture made my day.

I waved as he left, feeling almost giddy when, just

before he went around a building, he looked over his shoulder at me.

A foreign, sparkling feeling was rising in my chest. I'd been nineteen long enough to observe other boys this age. I knew that romances were many and fleeting and that this attention couldn't last. Still, it was a magical feeling, and I was grateful once again for this boy I barely knew.

I felt like I understood Elizabeth on a new level. She craved a physical connection, and she achieved it as best she could. Miaka spent hours typing to people on her computer or phone, wanting to connect intellectually That was what made them feel alive. Me? I'd been slaving away for the Ocean, hoping that at the end of it all, I'd find a romantic connection in my future life.

Truth was, there was no way to be sure I could get it. But as I sat there under the tree, something became clear. I wasn't worried. I wasn't sad. I wasn't even thinking that far into the future, because all I could think of was each minute with Akinli as it happened. Maybe the key for me to move forward wasn't to eliminate everything I was feeling; maybe all I needed to do was focus on the one feeling that made all the others seem small.

I pulled out my phone, laughing at how useless this thing was for me. I did research on it or distracted myself with it more than anything. Under my contacts were three numbers, and Aisling's wasn't even current.

I typed in the new one, fingers hesitating.

> Akinli? It's Kahlen. If you're still up for it, I'd love to make some cake this weekend.

I let out a long breath and pressed Send. I gathered my things to head home, brushing the grass off the back of my skirt.

Before I could make it to the edge of campus, my phone buzzed.

> I've got pans!

6

I lived for four days in a secret world of absolute bliss. I didn't sleep at all, because, for the first time in a long time, being awake was so much better. I spent hours looking up recipes, trying to find one that was a little above what a novice might make but wouldn't be too complicated for a dorm kitchen.

I could feel the weight of my sisters' stares as I hummed to myself. They didn't question the sudden lift in my mood, perhaps knowing I would remain close lipped. But when my giddiness didn't fade after a few days, I began to wonder how one boy was having such an effect on me.

I told myself that it was completely normal to think wonderful thoughts about someone whose last name I didn't even know. People had crushes on actors and musi-cians and celebrities they had absolutely no chance of meeting in real life. At least I'd planted my affections on someone who actually knew me.

I continually anticipated the next moment we'd be together, trying to keep the whole thing playful and light. I'd text, **You provide the oven and utensils, and I'll bring all the ingredients?**

He'd reply, **I will also bring my stomach. Because cake > actual food. Deal!**

How do you feel about cream cheese frosting? I'd ask.

It doesn't get enough respect, if I'm being honest, he'd say.

The days before our baking date were full of tiny notes like that, leaving me with an hour-long buzz from a single sentence. What made it better was that I didn't always have to start a conversation. By Wednesday, Akinli's questions were a little bit deeper and came to me unprompted.

So how long have you been cooking?

Feels like forever.

Did your mom teach you?

Actually, it's something I kind of picked up on my own.

☺

Smiley faces. He sent several. From anyone else, they'd seem ridiculous, but I felt pretty confident that if he typed one in, he was actually smiling.

Thursday we went most of the day without talking,

which I really didn't mind. I was in the middle of telling myself that I was making too much of this. Chances were that we'd have this one date, and he'd struggle so much with communicating that he wouldn't want to see me again anyway. And that would be for the best. After all, what kind of future could we possibly have?

This was what I was telling myself when, around ten that night, he sent me a picture of his very confused face with the words WHY MATH WHY? underneath. I lay in my bed laughing uncontrollably. First, he was just so, so, *so* cute! Second, he sent me a picture! I had a picture of a boy that he took just for me, and it felt bigger than anything I'd experienced in the last century.

There was a quick knock at my door, but Elizabeth and Miaka opened it before I could answer.

"You all right in here?" Elizabeth asked, perching a hand on her hip.

I took a deep breath and stopped giggling. "Yeah, I'm fine."

Miaka looked around the room. My TV was off, and there wasn't a book in my hand. "What's so funny?"

I picked up my phone. "Just something I saw."

"Can we see?" Elizabeth asked, reaching out.

I knew, if anything, they'd probably be happy I'd met someone. I just couldn't help but want to keep him to myself a little bit longer.

"Not sure you'd get it," I lied.

They shared a look, then eyed me suspiciously.

"Okay . . . we'll just go then." Miaka's gaze lingered on me before the door closed behind them.

I tightened my lips, trying not to laugh out of the pure joy of having a secret, then pulled up Akinli's picture again, smiling at his comically drooping eyebrows.

I searched through my phone for something to send back to him, maybe a picture of me in one of those dresses I loved. But I discovered that I had never turned the camera on myself. I had images of the sky, a bird, my sisters, but none of me.

I flopped down on my pillow, sweeping most of my hair above my head. Part of my face was buried in my comforter, but when I snapped the picture, it felt like an honest representation. I stared at that girl for a while, the giddy glow behind her eyes, the hint of a smile in her cheeks, and thought, *Yes, this is how this moment makes me feel.*

I sent it to him saying, **This is when you give up and get in bed. No one will care about your math grades in six years. Promise.**

I wanted to explain how many disasters I'd seen disappear in what felt like only minutes compared to the whole span of time.

Is it weird if I tell you you're pretty? he answered. **You're pretty.**

I thought of the way the water looked when I blew bubbles out of my mouth. That was the way I suspected it looked inside my body right now. Light and airy and bursting with happiness.

Is it also weird if I tell you I like talking to you even though you don't speak? I like talking to you.

"Where are you going?" Miaka asked the second my hand hit the doorknob the next night. I had really thought I was going to be able to sneak out without them noticing. Elizabeth's music was blaring from her room, and they'd been in serious dress talks for the last twenty minutes.

"Just for a walk. Might go by the store. You want anything?"

She looked me over, studying my outfit. Around the house, I enjoyed comfy rompers or sweaters, and if this had been an impromptu trip, I'd probably still be in those clothes. My skirt—which I already knew might be a bit much for the occasion but made me feel as nice on the outside as I did on the inside—was a bit of a giveaway.

"No. Nothing has sounded worth eating lately."

I nodded. "We should hit up a new state soon. Or a new country. Sometimes the smell of a different place will make me want to eat, you know?"

"I do! We should make some plans for where to go next. Sometimes our moves are too spontaneous for my tastes."

"Yeah," I said, shifting the weight of my purse. "A strategy would be good."

Miaka smiled and looked at my clothes again. "Well, maybe we can talk about a lot of things when you come back."

I said nothing but was sure my smile was as damning as my skirt. Oh, well. So much for secrets.

I got the groceries and lugged them all the way to Akinli's dorm, running slightly behind because I couldn't get into the building on my own. The university required ID cards to get into the dorms after six, and since I wasn't an actual student, I had to wait for someone else to come along and scan his so I could piggyback in.

"You need some help?" the boy asked, his eyes lingering on my mouth.

I shook my head no.

"Aww, come on. That's way too heavy for you."

He came closer, and again I cursed our natural appeal. I wasn't in danger exactly, and I knew that, but it didn't make these encounters any less uncomfortable. I shook my head again.

"No, really, which floor are you on? I can—"

"Hey, Kahlen!" I looked up to see Akinli walking down the hall. His button-up was open over the gray shirt beneath it, but I was thrilled to see that he'd at least put one on. "I was starting to worry. Hey, Sam."

"Hey." The boy gave Akinli a look and headed toward the stairwell, his displeasure at Akinli's arrival clear. In the meantime, I felt my mood lift significantly. I was now officially on my first date.

"Here, give me one of these." Akinli took a bag from my hands and led me to the elevator. "The kitchen's just up here. Now, I did some practicing this morning," he said proudly.

I raised my eyebrows.

"Yep. I made eggs. They were terrible."

I held in a laugh as the elevator dinged, delaying a moment before actually opening to the second floor.

"I think the problem was that I had no supervision, so this will probably go much better."

We turned into the small kitchen area, and I saw that he'd done some prep work. A whisk and a bowl were already out, as well as two different-size circular pans. He put down his bag and picked up another item.

"I took this off our door. My roommate was a pain about it, but if you need anything, just scribble it down." He passed me a whiteboard that had already managed to take a beating in the first few months of school. It was such a thoughtful gesture, I nearly cried.

I watched him as he carefully took out the eggs and sugar and flour, lining up everything along the back of the counter to give us room to cook.

"Is this almond extract? This is fancy. Again, I ruined food today, so remember, you're going to have to walk me through every step of this."

Wordlessly, I pulled out the printed instructions and laid them beside the bowl.

"There we go," he said, picking them up to study. He went over the multiple steps, his face looking more and more worried the closer he got to the end. He pulled himself together and peeked sheepishly at me over the top of the paper.

"Okay, Kahlen. Teach me to cook!"

7

Have you always lived in Florida?"

I shook my head and cracked another egg. It wasn't one of those things I could easily explain without speech. I waved my hand in a circle and made an exasperated face.

"All over the place?"

I nodded.

"Are your parents in the army or something? I only got to spend a year with one of my best friends in high school before his dad was stationed somewhere else. I hear that's pretty fast, though."

I watched him, listening intently, not really confirming or denying anything about my parents and hoping he wouldn't press any further.

"I grew up in this tiny town in Maine. Port Clyde. You ever heard of it?"

I shook my head, and he passed me the sugar he'd measured out. I took my finger and brushed the extra heap off the top into the sink.

"Oh, is that bad?" he asked.

Baking is science, I scribbled on the board.

"Huh. Okay, I will tuck that lesson away. So, yeah, Port Clyde. It's really small and mostly known for its lobster. There's also an artist residency there, so we get some creative types coming through town. That's why I thought you might have heard of it. You were drawing the other day, so I didn't know if that was something you were into or what."

I made a so-so gesture with my hand. Even with the whiteboard, it would be hard to explain that I really liked drawing because of my sort-of sister and that I wished I was half as good at seeing the world as she was.

"My parents are there, dying for me to come home. I'm an only child, so they're kind of lonely without me around. My mom calls me literally, like, every day. I told her she should get a puppy, but she said I was better than a dog, which is good, I guess. Am I talking too much?"

He paused, staring into my eyes, genuine worry coloring his face.

I shook my head. *No*, I thought, *I'd listen to you talk about nearly anything. You make phone calls sound like an adventure.*

"Okay. She's also worried because I'm still undeclared. I don't think that's a huge deal. Not yet anyway. Do you?"

I snapped my first two fingers and thumb together quickly, the ASL sign for *no*. Realizing he might not understand, I shook my head as well.

"Cool. What are you studying? Is it art?"

I didn't have another answer, so I nodded.

"You've got an artist vibe," he said knowingly.

I looked down at myself, then back up at Akniii, questioning him with my eyes.

"No, really. I'm not sure what it is, but you look like you've made and broken a lot of things and then made them all over again. Which makes no sense, I'm sure. But trust me, it's there."

I started whisking the batter. I was glad he didn't know how much I'd actually broken in my time—ships that cost millions of dollars, lives no one could put a price on—but I liked the idea that maybe, somewhere deep inside me, I was also capable of fixing things.

I passed the bowl to him, really hoping he'd participate.

"Oh, my gosh. Okay." He took the whisk in his hand. "I got this. Okay . . ."

He started whisking.

As he worked, I added in a few drops of the almond

extract, and after a moment he looked up at me. I tilted my head questioningly. *What?*

It took him a second to snap out of his stare. "Oh. Sorry. Nice teamwork there," he said, then winced as if he thought he'd said something dumb. "Speaking of team-work," he added, his voice lighter, "I think you could maybe help me with something."

I raised an eyebrow.

"Hear me out. See, if you're not talking, you spend almost every second of your life listening, taking things in, right?"

I nodded. That was all I did.

"I feel like, because of that, you're probably very per-ceptive. So as an experiment, I'd like to know what you think I should be studying."

I gawked at him.

You mean pick your major? I wrote.

"Exactly. I've had a few friends weigh in, but I think they were joking. Someone said musical therapy, and I've never so much as touched a kazoo."

I smirked at his exasperation.

"Come on. I need some direction in my life. Give it a shot."

I stared at this boy who I admittedly hardly knew. Yet I felt as if I'd learned so much about him, like, if anyone asked, I could outline his entire personality. He was so warm, so open, so full of simple joy. What had I done to catch his attention, to have him interested in not just my looks, but my thoughts?

I could tell he was actually eager to hear my opinion, so I focused on his question. I could imagine him as an advocate for an abused child or an aide for someone with mental illness, the only person in their whirlwind lives with the capacity to hold them down to the earth. I wrote on the whiteboard again.

"Social work?" he asked.

I applauded

He laughed, a sound more like music than anything I made. "I'm intrigued. Okay, Kahlen, I will research this field and get back to you." He glanced down at the cake batter, then raised the whisk and held it out to me, dripping. "Does this look right?"

I touched the whisk, then licked the batter off my finger. Akinli's warm blue eyes held mine as sweetness spread across my tongue. It was perfect.

I gave an enthusiastic nod, and he reached to taste it himself. "Hey, not bad for my first cake, yeah?"

I grinned. Not bad at all.

I greased the pans, excited that because they were two different sizes, we were going to end up with something that looked like a tiny wedding cake.

"I don't want to make a big deal about this or anything,

but I think it's kind of cool how you do everything you do."

I squinted at him.

"I mean, you use sign language, and it's hard to communicate. But you're into art and you can seriously cook and, for goodness' sakes, you can even jitterbug. By the way, I told my mom, and she wants a video. Totally doesn't believe me. But, yeah, I think it's nice that you don't let a little hitch in life slow you down. I admire that."

I smiled. For a minute, I admired myself, too. He didn't know how deep my problems ran, but he was right all the same. It was no small thing to *try*, to find out what you cared about in life. Even this moment, with this wonderful, temporary boy beside me, was a tiny miracle. I ought to give myself some credit.

I went to write my thanks but had a hard time getting more ink out of the marker.

"Ah, I thought it might die. You wanna come by my room real quick to get another?"

Stay calm, I thought. I nodded as nonchalantly as I could.

"Awesome. It's this way," he said with a wave, and I followed him down the hall. "I think my roommate left for a while, so at least you'll be spared that horror. I swear, it's like he took lessons in how to be an ass."

I grinned as we came upon a door with the obvious

blank space where the dry-erase board should be. On two little leaves that his RA had placed on all the doors down the hall were two names: Neil Baskha and Akinli Schaefer.

Schaefer. I longed to say it out loud. The shape of the word was so pleasant in my head, I couldn't wait to breathe it into the air. But that would have to wait until I was alone . . . and not distracted by the disaster that was his room.

To be fair, it was only half a disaster. It appeared that Neil's religious practices acknowledged neither trash cans nor recycling bins. Probably so he could build that haphazard altar of Mountain Dew cans by the window. Akinli's things seemed much homier. Instead of a store-bought comforter, he had a quilt. Instead of posters, he had pictures. Instead of beer cans, he had three bottles of Port Clyde Quencher root beer that he appeared to be saving.

He had said he was an only child, but there was a slightly older boy in a few of the shots who had the same eyes and chin. I saw his parents and one picture of him as a child holding a lobster in each hand and smiling so big I couldn't see his eyes.

"Here we go." He pulled out a new marker from his desk drawer, and I was drawn back from my quiet observations. "Sorry it's kind of messy in here," he said sheepishly, noticing my wandering eyes. "Neil . . . well, he's a character."

73

I smiled, trying to let him know I cared less about that than I did all the little pieces of himself I got to peek at, if only for a second.

Back in the communal kitchen, we played a game of hangman on the whiteboard between whipping up frosting and waiting for the cake to finish baking.

It was all so plain, so simple, and I was grateful for every single moment. When we managed to get both layers on—even though the top one wasn't quite centered—and covered the whole thing in buttercream, Akinli posed dramatically in front of our creation.

"The moment of truth. Have I overcome a long and difficult season of being the worst cook in America? Kahlen, the fork, please."

I passed it to him, picking up one myself so I could taste it, too. I didn't want to brag, but I was sure Aisling would be impressed.

"This. Is. Amazing!" Akinli yelled, taking two more heaping forkfuls before stopping to breathe. "We cannot keep something this beautiful to ourselves. Come on."

He picked up the plate and headed into the hall.

"Who wants cake?" he yelled.

A girl with her hair in two French braids stuck her head out of an open doorway halfway down the hall. "Me!"

Beside us someone opened his door, too. "What you hollering about, man?"

"We made cake!"

The guy's face turned from irritated to jubilant. "Cool."

Within minutes, half the floor had spilled out, using everything from spatulas to paper cups to get some dessert.

"I mean, I did an incredible job," Akinli said to someone, "but it was mostly Kahlen."

A few people patted my arm and thanked me for cooking or sharing. One girl said she liked my skirt. I wanted to burst, I felt so happy. Was this what it was like to be a normal nineteen-year-old girl? Living in a dorm, letting other peoples' lives spill over into yours, if only for a season? Studying one thing with absolute focus while having dozens of things change around you and learning from that, too? Having a boy see you, acknowledge you in such a way that you felt sure no one had ever experienced that feeling before, all the while knowing you'd joined a long line of people who did the same dance to find the person they spent their lives with.

It was timeless and temporary, important and inconsequential. And I got to be a part of it. I wanted to live like this all the time!

Then everything in my head slowed down. *All the time?* How was I supposed to manage that? After all the work it took to get through one date, how was I supposed to make it to ten? Or even two?

I watched Akinli, his smile lighting up the crowd, a

natural charisma floating around him. This had been special, beautiful even. But it wasn't sustainable. Eventually, something would rouse his suspicions. Why didn't I ever get hurt? Why didn't my weight ever change? Why did I have to disappear at random?

I felt so foolish. In the best version of this, he'd age while I didn't, and then when my time as a siren was over, I'd forget all about him.

It might be less painful if he simply forgot about me.

I backed slowly out of the crowd, so gifted at being silent that no one even noticed.

8

The girls weren't there when I got home, which was fine. Let them have one last night out in their vibrant, coast-side college town. I went to my room. Surveying the space, I realized there wasn't much I could actually call my own. There never really was.

I put the scrapbooks in my trunk, remembering I was still one person away from knowing the entire list of passengers on the *Arcatia*. I'd never forgotten about someone midsearch before. Sometimes I let them go when it was clear there was nothing to be found, but this was a first. Akinli had made me forget what I was for a little while, touched my skin like it was human, spoke to me like I was ordinary.

How magical it was just to be a normal girl.

There were a few pieces of clothing I liked, and a really nice wooden brush I had found at a flea market once. I had one rust-covered bobby pin that had been in my hair when I'd been changed, and I'd kept it because I assumed it was the same kind my mother used. It was the only thing I had left that tied me to her. There were a handful of other odds and ends, but my trunk was light when I pulled it to the front door.

The girls would see it when they came in. They'd know.

I went out the back and sat on the floating dock. I stared at the Ocean but didn't speak. I could hear Her, though, lapping up onto the shore and curving Herself around the wooden beams. I loved Her so much. She was home, the place where we could hide when wars raged or anyone looked at us with suspicion. She was life, our sustainer, *everyone's* sustainer. But now I couldn't help but be resentful. She was also the source of all my guilt, all my unmet dreams.

I had so many questions for Her. But not tonight.

I heard the familiar creak of the front door and headed back inside. Elizabeth and Miaka stood silent, staring at my trunk. Miaka looked on the edge of tears, and Elizabeth grumpily swung her strappy heels on the tips of her fingers.

"Why?" Miaka asked as I pushed the sliding door closed.

"I need to go." My tone was close to embarrassed, shamed by my weakness.

Elizabeth dropped her shoes. "Well, I don't. Neither does Miaka. We don't want to leave."

I avoided her glare. "I understand, but I can't stay here any longer."

"You always want to live somewhere big, somewhere we can be anonymous! Then you never even *try* to blend in. We're happy here!" When I peeked up at Elizabeth, the sharp set of her jaw solidified what I'd already guessed.

I took a shaky breath, then forced myself to speak evenly. "I'm fine going alone. Maybe you two would be better off without me. Aisling thrives in complete isolation, and it's possible I could, too. It's also possible that I would be completely miserable without you." I shrugged. "I really don't know. But if you want to stay, I understand. I'm taking my trunk to the car, I'm waiting thirty minutes, and, if you're in the car, then I'd be happy to have you along. If not, I'll see you when we sing."

I grabbed my things and took my keys out of my bag, walking past them. Once I was settled in the driver's seat, I pulled out my phone to check the time so I could actually give them the thirty minutes I'd promised, and saw I'd missed two texts.

They were both from Akinli. The first was obvious.

Hey, where'd you run off to? You okay?

And then:

Here's my problem. I've only gained two pounds of my freshman fifteen. Hoping you can help me out and we can try brownies next time? ☺

No mention of feeling brushed off. He even added a smiley face for good measure. Was it possible I'd run across the nicest person on the planet? A guy like him was as mythical as I was.

"Schaefer," I whispered into the night. "Akinli Schaefer."

It was as satisfying to say as I'd hoped.

As I looked back down to the phone, my fingers hovered. I wanted to reply, apologize maybe or explain that I had to move suddenly. But I knew that I couldn't let myself get drawn in.

I turned off my phone and inserted the key in the ignition to get the tiny clock on the dashboard up.

I watched the clock, and at twenty-nine minutes, my heart sank. I had no idea where I'd go. Beachfront was almost mandatory as we never knew when there might be an emergency, and it was easier, at least for me, if I could talk to Her from time to time. But now it was time to make a choice.

I swallowed and turned the key.

No sooner had the engine come to life then Miaka stuck her smiling face in the side window. "Pop the trunk for me? I had more art supplies than I thought."

I did as she asked, feeling guilty twice over. I'd told her earlier that we could discuss our move this time, and now I'd forced her to pack everything in thirty minutes.

She climbed into the front seat and sat beside me, pulling her hair up into a messy bun.

"I don't know why, but I thought you had something special happening. I thought you were getting comfortable here. I feel like I misread you completely."

"You're only ten years behind me," I said softly. "You know how this life takes its toll. I can't settle in. I try, I swear."

"I know." She put her hand on my knee. "You've stayed with us for decades as we've wandered freely. If you need a season of quiet, we can be there for you, too."

I rolled my eyes. "It looks like it's just you at the moment."

A split second later, the trunk slammed closed, and Elizabeth climbed into the backseat.

"I emailed the landlord, and we left cash for any cleaning he'll have to do. Let's go." She crossed her arms and threw on her sunglasses, even though it was dark.

I didn't say anything but smiled to myself. My sisters loved me.

I drove the whole way. After three hours, Elizabeth took over the music. After six, we saw the sun come up. After ten, we pulled into Pawleys Island and found an office that covered beach house rentals.

Seeing as it was the off-season and we were "awfully pretty," the rental agent didn't question three mute girls and our handfuls of cash.

By noon, we were settled into a thin, gray house at the end of the strip. The area was quiet, with a row of empty summer houses to the left and nothing but sand and beach grass to the right as far as we could see. It was perfect for getting into the Ocean and far enough away from town that I wouldn't have to see another soul if I didn't want to.

"It's quaint," Miaka said in admiration. "Can I have one of the beachfront rooms?"

"Fine with me." Elizabeth dropped her bags in the middle of the floor. "Okay, so this is home now," she said, eyeing the floral curtains and handwoven rugs with disgust.

"Just for now," I promised. "We won't stay forever."

She came over and wrapped her arms around me. "I'll make the best of it, for your sake. Maybe I'll learn to knit."

I pulled back to stare at her.

"What? I said maybe."

"Thanks for coming."

She sighed. "I really didn't have a choice. Miaka's like my other half, but I knew she wouldn't want to make you go alone. And I need you, too. I loved Miami, but not as much as I love you two."

"And I love you. I'd be lost without you."

"Oh!" she exclaimed suddenly, walking out of our embrace. "Movies!" Over my shoulder was a wall of films to entertain guests on rainy days. She loved movies and TV shows, so this at least might pacify her. For now anyway.

I looked out the large front windows at the Ocean. I'd settle into our new life, and then I'd go to Her.

Miaka moved the bed and dresser out of her room so she could turn it into a studio. "Fantastic light!" she said repeatedly. "Gorgeous!" Elizabeth complained that her room wasn't half as comfortable as the one in Florida, but she tried to fix the situation with new comforters and pillows and a willowy net she bought just to cover her bed. I even moved the TV out of my room and into hers as a gesture of thanks, and she seemed satisfied with the setup after a few days.

I took the other room with the Ocean view, and I watched Her. I didn't know what I was waiting for, but it was taking me time to find the will. Finally, after a week in our new home, I took my first steps across the sand and into the water.

Oh! You moved?

Yes, I thought. "I was having a hard time in the city. The others are with me."

83

What was so hard?

I shook my head and started to cry. "Everything."

I felt Her worry swelling, and I looked up and down the beach. It was late October, and the chill of fall was in the air. No one was rushing to the beach. I ran into Her, scared and sad.

Your thoughts are too fast, She said. *You must slow down.*

I'm just so confused, I confessed. *Why am I the only one who has nightmares? Even when I'm awake, these things haunt me. And why am I so afraid of humans? How can Aisling live alone without losing her mind? Why did You even pick me? I'm so confused. I'm so tired. . . .*

You're thinking way too much. One question at a time. We'll sort through this.

I hit my chest with my fist, accusing my body of failing. *I've had eighty years to adjust and never have. Am I broken?*

We'll start there. No. You're not broken. You are possibly the most loyal and faithful siren I've ever had.

So, one of the best? Is it bad to tell You that I don't really want to be good at this job?

She swirled around my face and hair, trying to console me. *No one with a beating heart could enjoy killing their own.*

I'm not human, I argued. *I'm less than that.*

Kahlen, my sweet girl, you are still human. Your body may be unchanging, but your soul still bends and sways. I assure you, in the deepest part of yourself, you are still connected to humanity.

I kept crying, my tears joining Her waves. *Then why can't I cope with any human contact? Elizabeth has had her lovers.*

As have many a siren before her. It's not surprising, considering how beautiful you are.

If it's so typical, then why can't I do that?

She laughed, a motherly sound in my head, as if She knew me better than I knew myself. *Because you and Elizabeth are very different people. She's looking for passion and excitement. In her dark world, those interludes are like fireworks. You long for relationships, for love. It's why you protect your sisters so fiercely, why you always return to Me even when I don't call, and why you mourn so heavily at taking lives.*

I considered Her words. I wondered how much of our past lives carried over with us. Elizabeth grew up in the era of free love; I grew up in till death do us part.

I fear this will always be a sore spot for you. You must become satisfied with the small circle of people you have. Even if you found someone who was your soul mate in every way, you could never stay with him.

Oh? I squashed everything about Akinli into the darkest corner of my mind, not wanting Her to know about the flicker of his life across mine. Then I felt silly for questioning what She said. The words were an echo of what I had thought when I'd left anyway.

There are the technical reasons why—that you would never age, that you might show your stronger-than-human qualities—but it also comes down to what you are.

A siren? I asked, the answer feeling too obvious.

No. Mine.

I felt my forehead furrow in confusion. I guess I'd always thought those were one and the same.

Why do you think there are only young women in My service? I cannot take mothers, and I cannot take wives.

I squinted, having never considered this before. *Why not?*

Wives will long for their husbands. Singing a song that primarily entices men is excruciating for a truly faithful wife. And to separate a mother from her child is the height of cruelty. I think any parent forced to endure a life permanently distanced from their child would lose their sanity. It wouldn't do for someone with that kind of agony to live this life. They could be volatile. That's dangerous for all of us.

But daughters? Daughters are meant to strike out from their families eventually.

True. I wrapped my arms around myself. *Though I don't think I had any great ambitions before. I'm not sure I do now either.*

Hardly the point. You're very driven. Eventually, you will find something to put all that energy into, and you will be unstoppable. Even now, with something you take no joy in, you do your tasks dutifully because it's all you can do. There's something beautiful in that, Kahlen.

I was slightly consoled by this, by the thought that there could be more in my future than I'd imagined. And even though it was difficult to accept praise in bringing death, I was proud that I'd never failed Her.

And I will answer your final question before you ask it again. I know you want to hear that there was something special about you or your sisters, that there's a method to all of it. But the truth is, I'm always aware of the time, how close the end is for any of My sirens. I was looking for someone, not knowing if there would be a girl on the ship or not. But of the five suitable young women on your ship, you cried out. When I spoke, you answered. So I took you.

That's it?

I'm afraid so.

It was a bit jarring to discover it was all so random, though I don't know what I was hoping to hear. As if She understood that, Her voice in my head softened, became even more affectionate. *However, this is something you need to know. While the choosing isn't driven by a specific desire for you, the life after you become Mine very much is. You are so prized by Me, you all are. And I don't want you to think your life has been wasted when it has been so precious to Me.*

I scrunched up my face in tears again, fearing that I'd somehow insulted Her with my questions.

Don't think that. I know your life is different from Mine. I accept you as you are.

I nodded, trying to take control of my emotions. *I'm just overwhelmed by it all.*

I know. And you may stay that way for the rest of your sentence. Don't let it ruin the time you have left with your sisters, with Me. We love you.

I nodded.

This has been a lot for one day. Go now. Go and live.

She gently pushed me toward the shore until the sand was sturdy enough under my feet that I could walk. It wasn't until I got to the bottom of the long porch steps that I let myself think about all that Her words meant.

The Ocean's possessiveness was obvious now more than ever, but despite all She had said, my mind kept returning to Akinli. In the past few days alone, it felt as if my affection for him had doubled, and he wasn't even near me. He'd been so extraordinarily kind. I kept telling myself this was a crush, a temporary, flighty thing that would pass as quickly as it came. But I missed him so deeply it hurt.

Then there was the worry over my sisters, the people who lived this life with me. I'd been unfair in uprooting them so quickly, but I hadn't known what else to do. Now we were here in this town on the edge of someplace big, but still distanced enough from everything that nothing exciting would happen for them here.

All I wanted to do was heal. I wanted to find a way to wrap myself up tightly enough so that the pain and sadness couldn't cut through. After talking to the Ocean, I wasn't sure that was possible. Maybe I had to exist in constant sadness.

She told me to live. . . .

I didn't know how to tell Her that simply being alive was not enough to be called living.

9

I kept to my room mostly. I kept waiting for something
to happen, which isn't how life works. In closed envi-
ronments, everything just repeats.

Elizabeth, of course, was the first to decide to head out.
After nearly a month of being cooped up in the house,
she finally came knocking on my door. "Miaka just sold
another piece. We're going shopping to celebrate. You
want anything?"

I shrugged. "Some tights maybe. And a sweater or two.
I can fake a winter wardrobe with those if I need to go
out."

"Is that something you plan on doing soon? Going out,
I mean?" She said it casually, but her eyes were sharp.

I turned back to my book. "I don't know. Not today."

"You sure? You can come and pick out your own tights. I realize that's just begging for trouble, but still," she teased.

I gave her a weak smile. "I'm fine here."

Elizabeth lingered in the doorway awhile, inhaling a few times as if she might argue with me but ultimately letting it drop.

"Okay then. We'll be back soon."

She left the door cracked, and I could hear her whispering worriedly to Miaka. "I tried to be nonchalant, but she says she wants to stay."

"She just needs time," Miaka whispered back. "Either something happened that she's not ready to tell us about, or she sincerely can't bear being a siren anymore. She's depressed."

"Well, how do we get her out of it? I can't live like this," Elizabeth hissed.

"She would do this for us. In a way, she has."

As low as their voices were, Elizabeth dropped hers even more. "Did you talk to Her? Did you tell Her how it's been?"

"The Ocean knows. She agrees that patience is the best path."

I closed my eyes. I knew I wasn't in the greatest mood at the moment, but I was surprised that they thought they needed a plan of action to deal with me. I couldn't believe they went to the Ocean.

I was a split second away from stomping out into the living room and telling them to mind their own damn business for once when I heard Her call.

Quickly! She urged. *Your new sister awaits. And she's very scared.*

I bolted out my door and out of the house, seeing that Miaka and Elizabeth were already on the move. I looked down the empty beach behind us, thankful that winter was coming and no one wanted to be near the water.

We ran into the surf, lifting our legs high until we were deep enough to be swept away.

Where are we going? I asked.

India. Be gentle with this one.

Of course.

Something about this felt similar to when Miaka had joined us, and that had me worried. Miaka had lived in a fishing village off the north coast of Japan. She never should have been on the boat in the first place, according to her sobs when we'd first come to her. She'd said she had told her family again and again how she feared the water and that she would do twice the work once everything was brought to land, if they'd only let her stay on shore.

They'd ignored her. They'd made her go out on the fishing boat.

And then they'd lost her.

I'd held on to a few things over the last eighty years: a vague memory of my mother's face, the knowledge that my father had a mustache, and the fact that I had two brothers, though I couldn't recall their names. But Miaka only remembered the name of her village and the details of her story because of us telling it back to her.

Elizabeth had held on to a lot, though it mostly seemed to be out of spite. She didn't like her family much, and it was as if she kept their names in her memory so she could curse them in her head. "See, Jacob. I traveled Europe. See, Mom. I've eaten delicacies. See, everyone. I did more than you ever could."

I didn't know what Aisling remembered. She'd never said.

But it was the thought of Miaka, so tiny and shaken after being swept overboard, that moved me so urgently to help this stranger; and even as fast as we moved, I wished it were faster.

Kahlen! I turned to see Aisling falling into place beside us.

Hey, I answered, worry in my voice. *It sounds like a bad one. We're going to have to be really careful this time.*

I think you should give the speech.

I turned to Aisling. *But I've never done it. You're the oldest. It should be you!*

I'll be gone so soon, Kahlen. It's only weeks now. She should

93

hear it from someone she'll have time to truly bond with.

I couldn't hide my nerves. It was a huge responsibility, to explain to our new sister what she would be signing up for.

Aisling laced her fingers through mine as we swam. *I'll back you up if you need me, okay?*

What she said made sense, though I was still scared of getting it wrong. But I couldn't let Aisling down. It was like the Ocean said: I put all of myself into a task.

Okay.

We focused ahead, searching the surface for the outline of a body miraculously set on the water as if it were a bed. Finally, the four of us slowed in the Arabian Sea.

Up there! Miaka said. We swam toward the girl, unsure how she would react to us. Shifting upright, we climbed into the air and were faced with the sickest sight I'd seen in my many, many years.

The girl wore a simple, plain sari. It had been torn in several places, and the damage obviously hadn't come from falling or some other little accident. It had been viciously ripped at. There were fresh bruises all over her arms and legs, but most horrifically, when we followed the trail of welts to her ankles and wrists, we saw there were cinder blocks tied to her, keeping her trapped.

"Untie the ropes. Hurry," I commanded, setting myself to undo a knot on her arm.

94

The poor thing weakly rolled her head in my direction, panting, still exhausted from her struggle.

"Please don't kill me." Her voice was shaking.

My heart ached. "No. We won't hurt you. Let us get these off so we can talk."

She nodded.

"Done," Elizabeth announced.

"Me, too." Aisling took the girl by her arm, helping her sit upright.

This girl, with her cinnamon skin and sleepy eyes, looked down at her blotched arms, touching several of her bruises as if she were counting. "Why?" she cried. "It wasn't my fault."

"What wasn't?" I asked, stroking her hair.

"Being a girl."

Miaka and Elizabeth came close, hoping to comfort her, but Aisling stayed back, focused on me. "What is your name?" I asked.

"Padma." She wiped at her runny nose.

"How old are you?" I tried to keep my tone calm and gentle.

She strained to think through her confusion. "Sixteen."

"Padma, what do you remember?"

She shook her head. "I don't want to remember."

I stroked her hair again, feeling the fear rise in her. "That's all right. But can you tell us how you got into the water?"

She looked around at us, a mixture of curiosity and shame on her face.

"Papa."

"I feel sick," Elizabeth whispered.

"Be strong. For Padma," Aisling urged. I, too, was moved to do everything I could to make this easy for her. This moment wasn't about any of us. It was singularly hers. Now I knew how Marilyn must have felt when she'd spoken to me and Miaka, how Aisling must have felt about Elizabeth. After everything, despite what was coming ahead, I just wanted this girl to live.

"He threw me in," she confessed, staring at her hands. "No dowry. A girl is too expensive. He beat my mother, then me. I don't remember how I got from my house to the water, but I can still feel the dock on my back. I woke up before he pushed me in. He didn't look sad at all."

I swallowed, composing myself.

I knew about Miaka's family's disregard of her fears. I knew Elizabeth's family didn't like her rebellious streak. But none of us had been through anything like this.

"Padma," I started gently, "I'm Kahlen. This is Aisling, Elizabeth, and Miaka." *Please let me explain this right*, I prayed. *Please let my words make her want to stay.* "We are very special young women, and we'd like to ask you to join us."

"Join you where?" Padma's gaze was wary.

I smiled. "Everywhere, really. We are singers, sirens. You might have read stories about us in books, or heard us mentioned in fairy tales. We belong to the Ocean. We sing for Her so She can live, so She can support the earth. Do you understand?"

"No."

Asiling laughed. "Neither did I."

"Me either," Elizabeth said, and Miaka nodded in agreement.

Padma smiled cautiously at us. "Your skin is so pale!" she breathed, amazed at Elizabeth.

"Yeah." Elizabeth held out her hand, and Padma ran her fingers across the palm until Elizabeth jumped back. "Sorry! That tickles!"

Padma let out a tiny laugh, looking down. She gasped, beginning to come to her senses. "Are we on water?"

I nodded. "We belong to the Ocean. If you choose to join us, you will be Hers as well. You won't age or be sick. You will stay just as you are for one hundred years."

I paused, letting her take that in. I wished I'd paid more attention to that detail when Marilyn changed me.

"For all that time, you will be a weapon of sorts. Your voice will be deadly, and you will have to keep it a secret, for all of our sakes. After those one hundred years pass, you will get your voice back, your life back. But until then, you serve the Ocean. You will never be alone. We'll take care of you, and the Ocean will, too."

"And my family?"

I shook my head. "I'm sorry, but you will never see any of them again."

Her face crumpled, and she cried openly.

"It will be okay," Miaka promised. "I missed my family once as well, but you will have an unimaginable life now."

"I don't want to go back to them," Padma blurted. "If joining you means staying away from my family, I'll take it. I'm so grateful to get away!"

Aisling and I smiled at each other.

"So you'll stay with us?" I asked.

She looked up, her eyes wide. "Yes! Oh, yes! Please take me away!"

"Can we stay with her?" I asked the Ocean. "For the change?"

Yes, I think that's wise.

"What was that?" Padma asked.

"We have much to explain. But, for now, you need to come underwater. There's a little of the Ocean inside you now so that you can hear Her, but She needs to finish in order to keep you."

Padma was nervous, but she nodded all the same.

"Watch Elizabeth."

My wild sister rose, took a few steps, then jumped

gracefully into the Ocean as if she were simply hopping off the curb of a street.

"See. Nothing to it. Let's go." I stood, and Miaka, Aisling, and I escorted Padma under the water.

Adorably, she held her breath.

We swam around her, never letting her feel alone, as the Ocean opened Padma's mouth and forced a strange, dark liquid down her throat. I had no idea what it was exactly, or where it came from, but I knew the very same water was running through my veins, mingling with my blood, keeping me alive. And I knew that magic hung suspended in my lungs and throat, making my voice so deadly.

Padma's bruises healed over, her skin grew luminous, and without aging a day, she suddenly looked like someone who had spent years figuring out who she was and had comfortably settled into herself.

When the Ocean was done, Padma hung in the water, a little jittery as she relearned how to breathe.

"Let's go." Miaka grabbed her hand and pulled her toward home.

We watched as her ragged sari fell away, and I assumed she mustn't have felt it, seeing as she didn't go to cover herself. But she did notice when the salt stuck to her, creating her very first siren dress.

As we walked out of the water to return to our house, Padma held out her arms, looking at herself.

"I have been reborn! I am a goddess!"

She was radiant, laughing as Miaka and Elizabeth led her and Aisling into our house.

Keeping my feet in the water, I thought, *You made a good choice.*

It was a difficult call, in all honesty. She was torn about living.

"Because she thought living meant returning to her family?"

I suppose. The images in her mind were gruesome at best. Her father you already know about, but her mother always kept her distance. It was like . . . Padma was a crime she was guilty of, and she wanted to remove herself from her daughter as much as possible.

"I can't imagine any mother behaving that way. I hope she's already forgetting."

It seems that way. You're all different, but I would guess she'll let it all go if she can.

I walked along the coast, my feet in the water as I stood in front of our beach house, watching the shadows of my sisters as they moved around the living room. I felt thankful that Padma had chosen to come with us, interested in my new sister in a way I hadn't been interested in anything since we'd left Miami.

"I have a question. Was this solely for her?"

What do you mean?

"Did You guess she would wake me up?"

I hoped.

"I hope, too."

"Kahlen!" Elizabeth called, and I tried not to panic about her voice going out so freely in the air. There was no one in sight, but that didn't mean there was no one in earshot. Voices carried. "Padma is trying to steal a pair of your shoes already!" She laughed with delight, and I sighed, so happy that Padma was falling into step with us as if she'd been here all along.

"Tell her she can have anything she wants."

10

O ur small house was suddenly full to the brim.
Elizabeth took Padma under her wing, thrilled
to finally have a younger sister, and Aisling
stayed with us instead of returning to her cottage, since
her days as a siren were now so few.

We spent the first night around a bonfire Miaka made,
drinking delicious coffee and exposing Padma to the wonderful world of s'mores.

"But we don't *have* to eat?" she asked yet again.

"No," Aisling explained. "Lack of food, water, or sleep
will not harm you at all. We indulge in them sometimes
for fun, but you don't need them."

"And I can't get hurt?"

"Nope," Elizabeth said excitedly. "Look at this." She walked over to the fire and stuck her hand directly into the flame. I turned my eyes to Padma, watching the disbelief on her face even as she saw it happening.

"Do you even feel anything?"

Elizabeth shrugged, pulling back her hand. "I can tell it's hot, but it doesn't hurt. It's hard to explain."

Padma looked delighted. "So I can't get a cold? A fever? Anything?"

"No." I laughed. "You are a superhero. Maybe a super-villain," I added, not really sure. Padma's arrival had made me so happy, the thought didn't bring me down. "Either way, you're strong and safe now. A fever is a joke to us."

She sighed. Just as we all had, she'd refused to take off her first sea salt dress, touching the beautiful, shimmering folds. "I once had a cut that got infected, and I had a fever for days. I thought I was going to die. I remember when I woke up, drenched in sweat after it broke." Padma shook her head at the memory. "It's hard to imagine that being impossible now."

I glanced at Aisling, who had the same questioning look in her eyes.

"Padma, that's a very specific memory," Aisling said slowly.

She shrugged it off with a smile. "It was very scary. Hard to forget."

"But that's the thing," I said, touching her arm. "Most

103

sirens forget their pasts incredibly quickly. I can't remember the names of anyone in my family, let alone a particular day I was sick."

Elizabeth piped up. "It was a struggle for me, but I remember their names. I even kept tabs on my family for a bit. They were never really keen on me being less than a lady, and every once in a while, I'd find out something about them, like that my parents finally got divorced and my brother flunked out of law school. It was validating, like they weren't perfect either."

I stared at Elizabeth. We all knew why she held on, but she'd never told us these particular details. I wondered what it was about Padma that made her share it with everyone. Now I knew that Elizabeth had kept a mental scrapbook, and that was something I understood very well.

Aisling tilted her head. "All we're saying is, even a few hours in, it's unusual for you to still know that detail about yourself."

Padma looked into each of our eyes, worried. "So am I not healthy? Not like you?"

"How did you get that cut you had on your arm?" Miaka asked.

Padma barely paused to think. "Papa. He hit me with a pan."

Miaka nodded as if she'd assumed this was the case. "You've been through a lot, Padma. More than any of us, that's for sure. But you can let that all go. He's never coming to get you, and if he does, he won't survive."

Padma's face scrunched together, and she buried her face in her hands as the tears came. I immediately moved closer to hold her, and the others came as well.

"I don't want to remember," she whimpered. "I don't want to remember anything before today."

"Don't worry," I whispered. "It will all go away. And we're here for you until it does."

I felt her shoulders slump in release, as if that was so much more than she could have hoped for.

"We travel," Elizabeth promised. "You'll get to see the whole world."

"And we try the best foods," Aisling added, smiling encouragingly.

"We've all learned sign language, so we can communicate even in a crowd. We'll teach you. Everything is going to be all right now." I stroked her hair as she nodded, accepting our words like gifts.

It had been a long time since I thought about just how sacred this sisterhood was, how we would be there for one another as long as our service lasted. Today was the first time in a while that I found myself grateful for it.

Padma adjusted a little better over the next few days, and I stepped back to let Elizabeth and Miaka have their hand in teaching her. I sat on a dune with Aisling as my other sisters showed Padma how to talk with the Ocean. They had their feet in the surf, and I could see them using gestures to explain how She could call to you wherever you were but how we needed contact to speak back. Luckily, contact could come through many things. Falling snow, a mud puddle, and even dense enough fog could carry our words to Her.

"I've never seen them be so responsible." I fiddled with the sea grass in the dry sand just in front of one of those tiny fences that helped stop the wind from sweeping it all away.

Aisling laughed. "I think Padma's sorrow makes them minimize their own. Not that their sadness or regrets don't matter, but her heartbreak draws them near."

"I feel like I've been greedy. We knew that Miaka was mistreated and that Elizabeth's family acted like she'd never amount to much. This second life has been a blessing for them, and I treat it like a prison."

"It is in a way," she said heavily.

"But it's worse for me. Or at least I feel like it is."

"Why, do you think?"

I shook my head. "My life wasn't like theirs. My family was well off. Even when everyone else was losing money, we were making it. And I was always treated like someone special." I squinted, trying to grab at long-lost thoughts. "I

106

was the oldest, the only girl. I feel like there were expectations, but nothing that upset me. I think we were happy. Mostly."

"I'm sorry you've been so unhappy since," she said quietly.

I sighed, staring out at the Ocean.

"Kahlen, I've known you the longest. I've seen you cry for days after some of our singings and wake up from nightmares clawing at the air. I've watched you draw in when others flourish." She shook her head. "I have a few weeks. She said that since the next singing is still months away, I can go as soon as I like. I asked for some time to say good-bye to you all, to help Padma adjust, and to prepare."

I blinked back my tears. "I can't believe you'll be gone so soon." The joy I had at gaining a new sister was on par with the pain of losing another.

"I know. It's almost scary for me not to do this anymore." She swallowed. "But that's beside the point. Kahlen, I want more than anything to help you find hope in this life, to have as much happiness now as you did before we'd met. What can I do? I don't want you to spend the next twenty years suffering when you might be able to do something remarkable."

I felt my eyes stinging. "It's not just the work. That's bad enough, but . . . I . . ."

Aisling wrapped her arm around me. "Please tell me

what's going on. I won't judge you or break your confidence. Whatever it is, you clearly can't carry it alone."

I looked at my sister, wondering if I could finally confess what had been pressing on my heart for weeks. I'd pushed Akinli so far down in my mind, feeling as if the only way to dull how much I missed him was to make him as small as possible. But here, finally, was a chance to speak. Aisling would be gone soon, and this memory would go right along with her.

"I've been guarding this," I confessed. "I don't want the others to know."

"If you need someone to tell your deepest, darkest secret to, trust me, no one could keep it better than me."

I nodded. "There was a boy."

Aisling laughed. "Honey, plenty of sirens have boys."

"No," I said. "Not a passing affair . . . I think I'm in love."

"Oh." Her face fell. "Oh, Kahlen."

"I know." I curled into a ball on the dune, feeling foolish. "I told myself it was just a crush. It all started and ended in ten days. How could that be anything close to love? But I think about him every day. I banish him from my mind when I go to the Ocean, because I know what She'd say."

"No mothers, no wives. She wouldn't want you to fall in love," Aisling said, something bitter in her tone.

"Exactly."

There was silence for a moment, nothing but wind and the crash of waves. I knew Aisling wanted to help, but what could she do? I knew the rules.

"Don't tell me his name, but tell me about him. Why do you think you're in love?"

I smiled without thinking about it. "Have you ever had someone see you? Like, really see you? I know people are drawn in by our beauty, but it was as if he bypassed that altogether. He made me feel like all the bad I'd done was erasable, that there was something good in me. And nothing got in his way. Aisling, I'm telling you, he worked around my silence. He would guess at things I might say and answer in turn, or find a way to make sure I'd be able to communicate.

"The worst part . . ." I pursed my lips, not wanting to cry. "The worst part is that in twenty years, I'll forget I even had this feeling. And if I could get it again, I'm not sure I'd want it with someone else. I know it's ridiculous to think that something so brief could be so life changing, but I swear, it feels real."

Aisling brushed her hand through my hair. "I believe you. I fell in love once in a matter of minutes."

I chuckled. "How could you even remember?" I stared at Aisling, wide-eyed in disbelief. "Do you . . . do you have a lover?"

"No," she said firmly. "I have a daughter."

I was speechless.

"Well, I had a daughter." Aisling smiled at the memory. "And then I had a grandson, who is doing very well in his old age. And now I have a great-granddaughter." Her eyes brimmed with happy tears. "She happens to bear my name."

I shook my head. "How . . ."

"I'm private. Even in my own head, I'm guarded. When my ship went down, I fought for my life, but I think I wanted to protect Tova so much that she was hidden too deep in my thoughts for the Ocean to see. I didn't think of anything but surviving then. Later I mastered keeping the secret from Her by pushing thoughts of Tova away when I was with Her, just like you've done with this boy. And because I wanted so much to hold on to Tova, I didn't forget her."

Aisling beamed, proud of keeping this monumental news to herself for a century.

"Were you married?" I guessed, still in shock.

"No," she said flatly. "Tova's father didn't stick around. He said he loved me, but the moment I told him I was pregnant, he disappeared. I don't remember his name anymore." She swallowed, pulling her memories together.

"My parents turned me out, ashamed. I was sent to live with my aunt and uncle in the north. They had no children and were pleased to have me, even though I'd been disgraced. And when Tova came"—Aisling sighed—"she made the whole world brighter. I was glad her father didn't want her, because it meant she was all mine."

Her joy turned to sadness almost instantly. "I'd gotten a letter from my parents, wanting to make amends. Tova and I were going to travel by steamer and, I hoped, be reconciled with my family. I knew once they saw how beautiful she was they'd adore her. So the plans were all set . . . Then Tova got sick. She seemed healthy enough by the time we were supposed to leave, but I didn't want to risk having her travel before I was sure she was fully recovered. Easily the best decision I ever made."

"So she lived?"

Aisling nodded. "She grew up with my aunt and uncle. I don't know why my parents didn't take her. It's not as if I could ask. From time to time, I'd go back, wear my hair under a kerchief or dress as an old lady. I watched my daughter grow up and fall in love and have a family. I've had her whole life, and I couldn't ask for more. Well," she amended, "I shouldn't ask for more."

Aisling stared into the sand, seeing years and years of other people's lives contained within her own. She was, I thought, quite possibly the most extraordinary siren that had ever lived.

"I'm telling you this for several reasons. First, so you

will understand my departure plan and see it through to the end. Second, so you can trust that I will take your secret out of this life with me. And third, so I can explain to you what you must do next."

I didn't dare hope that there was a way to get back to Akinli, but if Aisling had done all that she'd just told me, maybe there was a chance.

"The Ocean says She doesn't take wives. She says She doesn't take mothers. I've been a mother, a grandmother, and a great-grandmother; and I've never failed at serving Her."

I absorbed those words, seeing the last eighty years in a new light. Aisling had never forgotten her own past. She had kept the attachments of her human life, taken time away from us so that she could follow her daughter's life, and yet she'd performed her work so flawlessly that the Ocean had never questioned her devotion. Aisling was proof the Ocean wasn't always right.

"If this boy is that important to you, you have to take what you can get. You might not be able to be with him again. You might have to endure him marrying someone else. But you can go and see him. Dye your hair from time to time, dress like you're older than you are. It is possible to watch someone without being seen. Let him live his life and be happy for him. If you can be satisfied with that, then find a way. If not"—she shook her head—"then please, for everyone's sake, let him go."

I nodded, knowing she truly understood.

"Thank you, Aisling. You've changed everything."

"Tell no one."

I took her hand and held it in mine, promising. "Never."

11

On Christmas Eve, the Ocean took us all back to Sweden with Aisling, just as she wished. She wanted to spend one last night in her tiny cottage that she loved so much before being changed back. Then the others and I would set her up in her new life as best as we could. There were no guarantees once she was human again.

"So we'll leave the bed for you for tonight," Miaka said. "And those are the clothes you picked out?"

Aisling looked over to the small, leather backpack she'd set in the corner and the clean dress and tights she'd hung up just above it. "Yes."

Her voice was meek, tired.

"Why are you so down?" Elizabeth asked, twirling to admire the shimmer of her sea salt dress. "You should be celebrating, right? It's Christmas, and you're getting the best present ever! Aren't you excited?"

Aisling nodded. "Of course. It's strange is all."

"I'm going to start cooking," Miaka said. "I think a final meal will do us all good."

"Can I help?" Padma asked, clearly looking to find a way to fit into the group. I imagined this was difficult for her, attending the departure of a sister she'd only known for a few weeks.

"Of course," Miaka replied. "I'm putting everyone to work!"

"Not Kahlen," Aisling said. "I need her for a moment."

"Sure. Whatever you want."

Aisling and I changed out of our sea salt dresses and into something more conventional before stepping outside. I could see her taking care with each movement, as if she were studying herself.

She put on tall boots and gloves and even a hat, encouraging me to do the same. I knew then that I might be delving into more of her secrets. The snow was merely frozen water, natural water, that all linked back to the Ocean. A rogue toe in a mud puddle was enough for us to communicate with Her, whether we needed to or not. Today, She was going to be out of our touch until Aisling decided differently.

Our breath hung in the air as we stood under the canopy of branches that shielded the little house. Aisling was still, her face tensing more and more by the moment "So, what do you need me for?" I asked.

She swallowed, trying to maintain her smile. "Someone has to know where to take me. Come, I have a few details to tend to along the way."

Aisling didn't seem to want to speak, so I followed her in silence, the crunch of our shoes on the snow the only sound. We walked for quite a while before I started seeing signs of the town, a rural area just in from the coast. We passed small houses attached to large farms first, then a few shops and some apartment buildings, and finally came to a beautiful town square.

After all the large cities in which we'd lived, it was hard to believe a place this quaint and rustic was real. Twinkle lights were hanging from trees, and the small shops had decorations in their windows. Children ran down the street in their wool coats, singing carols as if they were battle cries. The scent of cinnamon and citrus filled the air, and I was glad this was the way I'd see Aisling's final home.

I got her attention and signed to her. "I can see why you like it here."

Her face was still tinged with sadness. "Part of me fears I won't like it after."

"Nonsense. This is you."

Near the edge of town, Aisling gave me some money and asked me to go into the corner shop for flowers. I was confused by the request but did it all the same, returning with dark-red flowers I didn't know the name of. She thanked me and took them, marching onward, out of the bustle of the town.

Aisling walked with sure steps, knowing the path well. I followed her at a distance, sensing this was hallowed ground. As we came upon the graveyard, she paused, her hand on the post, collecting her strength before carrying on. There were other footprints in the snow, proof of families visiting their kin on this very special holiday. When she came across the slightly weathered headstone, she stopped, picked up the dried flowers that presumably she'd brought on her last visit, and set the new ones in their place.

I studied the dates and realized Aisling's daughter had been dead twenty-six years. I tried to remember exactly what we were doing then. Did Aisling ever let it show that she'd just gone through the most devastating thing a mother could? How did she keep living when Tova was gone?

After a few moments of silence, Aisling's shoulders began to shake. She looked around nervously, and I did the same. We were alone. When she was finally sure of it, she let out an anguished cry, and I rushed over to wrap my arms around her.

"It's okay, Aisling. She got to live her life. She got that because of you."

"I'm not sad that she's gone," she wept, wiping her tears with the back of her hand. "I'm sad because after tomorrow I won't even know that she lived."

She let out a pained, guttural moan, doubling over and grasping her daughter's gravestone. I realized then that in the last hundred years, this was the closest she'd ever been to holding her child.

And she'd never do it again.

I had always thought forgetting would be a blessing, but now, for Aisling's sake, I wished a little could stay.

A familiar word caught my eye, and I turned to the stone on one side of Tova's. It marked the short life of Aisling Evensen. I wondered what her family had put in there to represent the girl they'd lost.

She brushed off her face and smoothed out her hair. "I just wanted to tell her I loved her one last time."

"If your great-granddaughter is named after you, then I'm sure she always knew."

Aisling smiled a bit. "Thank you."

She leaned her head into mine, and we stayed like that for a minute. I couldn't begin to imagine all the thoughts going through her head, and my only hope for the rest of her life as a siren was to make everything simple and painless.

"I'm ready," she whispered.

We stood together and started walking. Aisling didn't look back.

"There's a boarding school in town. I want to be left there."

"At a boarding school? Are you sure?"

"Yes." She kept her eyes straight ahead as she spoke. "You'll need to write a letter for me, explaining why you had to abandon your sister. But I've got enough money saved for two years of tuition, which is more than I need. I'm hoping that the town will just accept me as one of their own by the time I graduate, and then I can find a job working here."

I considered her plan. It seemed so . . . ordinary.

"Do you not have any other passions or pursuits? Isn't there anything else you want?"

She shook her head. "My great-granddaughter teaches at that school. All I want is to have a chance to be one of her students, and live and die where my family did. Anything after that is more than enough."

"Did you really hide yourself so well all this time that no one will notice?"

Finally, she laughed. "I spent plenty of time away with you all, and I've lived in other places. I've visited this area only once or twice a year. Not to mention that I've rein-vented myself more than you could guess. Besides, the town's not so small that everyone knows everyone. Stay out of the way, and it's easy to blend into the background."

"You'll make quite the Christmas surprise," I mused.

She smiled. "I see the girls there, and some of them seem sad to be in the same place all year. They don't have anywhere to go for the holidays. I think it will actually be fun for them, someone new showing up on Christmas. And once they all hear my story, it might give them something to be grateful for."

"How do you mean?"

She shrugged. "I'll be the girl with no family. Whatever they're going through, it will be better than that."

There was something close to pride in her voice, as if she was happy to give this to others despite knowing how people would talk.

"I'm really impressed, Aisling. With your plans, with how you've lived your life. I can't believe this is possible."

"Now you know it is," she replied with a smile. "Speaking of which, have you made any decisions about attempting something like this yourself?"

"No, not yet. I feel like if I tried, I could be as clever as you, but I'm not sure I could be as strong."

She wrapped an arm around me. "You have more strength than you know. Trust me."

We got closer to town and fell silent. Aisling pointed out the boarding school, noting which door we should use. The school was actually kind of pretty, with its white walls and tall windows. A few girls sat on the steps in their uniforms, braving the cold with cups of steaming cider, and I pictured Aisling in that spot, laughing with friends. I hoped she would never be sad about waking up without her memories.

For her sake, I tried to infuse the night with as much happiness as I could. We didn't give her presents, knowing she couldn't take much with her, but we filled her up with food before we all walked into the Ocean together.

Good-bye, Aisling. You served Me so well.

I'm happy You think so, she answered, her voice full of gratitude. *And thank You for this astonishing life. It was more than I could have asked for.*

You're welcome. Are you ready?

She swallowed once. *Yes.*

Close your eyes.

She did, but they jerked open a moment later as the liquid was forced out of her. Aisling writhed, gripping at her neck as if she were trying to fight off strangling hands. Her arms and legs flailed violently until she finally went limp, and the girls and I swam to rush her unconscious body out of the water.

Headmaster Strout,

Please take care of our beloved sister, Aisling. For reasons we cannot articulate here, we have been forced to part ways. In her bag you will find tuition money, and once she is enrolled, we are sure you will find her to be a bright, diligent, and excellent student. We realize this request is a bit unorthodox, but please, we beg you, see it through. This is the best that we can do for her.

And to Aisling, our guide and strength, please move forward in life knowing that you are loved beyond anything most souls would know. We wish you every happiness in life and hope you will walk on in complete and unspoiled joy.

You are in our hearts always.

Love, Your Sisters

12

The others went back to the Ocean, but I stayed, watching from the shelter of a group of trees near the school until Aisling woke up. It was before dawn when she stirred, clearly disoriented. She cried a little, and eventually someone heard her. She clutched herself tightly as an older woman walked her into the school.

Once she was safely inside, I started walking. The cemetery was deserted on Christmas morning. I knelt in front of Tova's grave and pulled a few flowers out of the bouquet we'd left her the day before. I didn't think she'd mind sharing with her mother.

I left them on Aisling's grave, knowing now that this girl was truly gone. I pulled up my hood as a fresh snow began to fall and made my way to the Ocean.

Swimming back to South Carolina felt lonely. I'd already seen Marilyn and Nombeko go through their changes, but this time felt different.

Of course it does, the Ocean said, reading my thoughts. *She's been with you the longest. It'll be the same for Miaka when she does this for you.*

That makes sense, I allowed. *It's just that it feels like we're missing something now.*

She kept to herself so much, I'm sure once you get home and get back to teaching Padma, it will feel as if nothing's changed.

I hope so.

At home, everyone was in a jolly mood and doling out presents to one another.

"You have a pile over here," Miaka crowed, begging me to join.

"I know, and I have some for you, too. But I need to get into dry clothes. Save me some cookies."

"I can't promise that," Elizabeth yelled.

I chuckled and went into my room to shower and change, trying to shrug off my sadness over losing Aisling and prepare myself for everything to come. It was Christmas, after all, so I decided to give myself one tiny present.

Digging my phone out of my faithful wooden trunk, I powered it up for the first time in months.

I was thrilled to see I had messages waiting.

Akinli's two texts from our last night together were still there, but there were others after it. The first one was a few days later.

Cake girl! You there? Sorry if I did something wrong. Come by the library sometime.

That one sent a pang of guilt through me. I hated him thinking my leaving was his fault. He'd been nothing but kind. Heaving a sigh, I moved to the next one.

Hey, you there? Could use a good listener right now. Text if you can.

I considered that one for a while. I liked listening to him when he talked about the inconsequential, and I wished I had been there to listen to him if he truly needed it. I swallowed, moving on.

Sorry, know this is random. Had cake today. It was crap.

Anyway, hope you're doing ok.

That was the last one, dated about a month ago. I smiled at the words. I was glad it was only five messages and not one for every day we'd been apart. It was enough to show he thought of me from time to time. Maybe he'd remember me down the road, whatever life he lived, as that girl he'd met one time who he baked a cake with and who knew how to jitterbug.

My heart lifted at the thought. That last night, in the dorm hallway, I'd thought it would be easier if he forgot me before I forgot him. Now I had a sense that even after his name and face were wiped from my mind, there was a chance I wouldn't be wiped from his.

In the weeks after Aisling left, things did begin to get back to normal, but not in the ways I had hoped. While I found myself loving Padma, just as I loved my other sisters, the novelty of her presence in the house wore off, and I began to spend more and more time in my room again, alone. Honestly, there were days when her mood seemed as somber as mine, and being in her presence only magnified my anxieties.

I tried not to think of the singing, which was so close now. I could feel Her pain, Her aching hunger. She would hold off as long as She could, for our sakes, but it wouldn't be much longer.

I tried to forget about the future and threw myself into research, scouring the internet for the last passenger of the *Arcatia*, and I finally found him: Robert Temlow, fifty-three, an insurance salesman. A picture of his thin, tanned face went into my scrapbook, completing a passenger list for the first time. I closed the book, thinking I'd feel something. Accomplishment, satisfaction. But nothing came.

It was a familiar emptiness.

One of my first research projects had been on sirens, when I had been with my sisters for only a few years. I had tried to learn everything I could about my new life. I dug out those old notes and went through them once again.

I had found a wealth of art and more short stories than I would have imagined, and in general there was some truth to many of the pieces. In several places, the number of sirens was said to be two, in others five, and those were indeed our limits. It was almost an impossible job to do alone, but having too many at once increased our chances of exposure.

A lot of what I read was absurd. I rolled my eyes at the descriptions of women with the bodies of birds, flinched at the artists who turned us into fetishes. But then I thought of Elizabeth, quietly luring boys into bed, and knew it wasn't completely far-fetched.

Nowhere did it mention how we served the Ocean or that sirens didn't exactly want to be in this position. No one explained how it all began. There wasn't a single piece that advised how to escape from this sentence. I had been so desperate in the beginning, longing for some kind of answer. The Ocean became the only truth I knew. Nothing made sense but Her.

I pushed my notes away and flung myself into the oversize chair in the corner, looking out at the water. I found myself missing Aisling, which felt silly after us being apart most of the time anyway. Maybe it was just because, for a small period of time, she was the only one who understood what I was feeling. She made me feel less isolated in my sadness.

As I stared at the breaking waves, I found myself wondering if Akinli was doing the exact same thing right now. He said he grew up in a little fishing town in Maine. Port Clyde. Maybe at this very moment, he was sitting with his parents, drinking hot chocolate, and watching sleepy waves roll in. Or perhaps they were finishing up those holiday trips to see extended family that everyone seemed obligated to take this time of year. I was willing to bet he was wearing a hideous sweater from some great-aunt just so he wouldn't hurt her feelings.

Or maybe he was already packing, getting ready to head out of the blustery winter up north to the milder weather of Florida. Maybe he'd picked a major by now and was so excited to get back to school, he couldn't stand it. I wonder if Neil had gotten any easier to live with or if he was still making trash sculptures in the corners of their room.

Maybe, just maybe, once in a while he would go by the tree we sat under, waiting to see if I'd show up. . . .

I was so tired of crying. So tired of salt water. But it seemed unavoidable. If I wasn't going to swim in it, it would flood out of my body instead.

I wanted to go to him so bad. I felt like I owed him an apology for leaving the way I did, for not having my phone on that one time he needed to talk, for walking into his life in the first place. And it hurt feeling this growing, heavy thing in my chest for him and not knowing if any of it was reciprocated.

It was all too much at once. Aisling was gone, but I still needed to keep her secret. I had a new sister who seemed as stuck in her past life as if it was still happening. I loved and hated the Ocean at the same time. And I missed Akinli so deeply that it weighed down my unbreakable bones.

I turned away from the Ocean, tucking myself into bed. I didn't need to sleep, but I wanted everything to stop for a while.

When I woke after a mercifully dreamless sleep, I could hear my sisters discussing me in the living room.

"It's not you she's avoiding," Elizabeth said, and I could tell from the gentle note in her voice that she was talking to Padma. "She just gets like this."

"She's served the Ocean longer than any of us," Miaka added. "It's hard for her. We just need to give her space."

Climbing out of bed, I looked at the floral-patterned curtains, the bland pictures on the walls of my room, and suddenly hated them. This house felt like a trap. I'd fled here to get away from my hopeless love for Akinli, but I hadn't gotten away from myself.

I opened the door of my room, and my sisters fell silent as I came to join them. Miaka and Elizabeth looked embarrassed, and I knew they were wondering if I had overheard them discussing me.

"I think it's time to move again," I told them.

13

The New Year came and went, just the same as all the others, and no ships sank. February came, and no tsunami swept anyone into the Ocean. March passed, and there were no floods. As we crossed into April, the inevitability of singing again became more and more real, and that familiar dread filled my body. The Ocean could hold back between shipwrecks for a year at most, Her hunger increasing with each full moon, and it had been almost a year now.

I bought a brand-new scrapbook, and braced myself. I heard the Ocean's hunger in every crash of a wave, every hiss on the sand. It felt like an ache in my own body, which made sense as She was actually in me. But yearning to ease that pain in myself did nothing to make the coming singing any more desirable.

"Where would you want to go, Elizabeth? You haven't picked anywhere in a while," Miaka offered. True to my word, this time we were planning before we found a new home.

"I'd go back to Miami, but I'm assuming it's out of the question." She eyed me.

It was spring, so he'd be back in school now. I could wear my hair under a hat and buy some blue jeans. If I stayed far enough away, he'd never notice. But how could I stay away?

"I don't think that'd be a good idea." I scribbled circles on the pad of paper we were using to brainstorm. I couldn't even put down the name of the city.

"What's in Miami?" Padma wondered.

"Beaches," I answered quickly. "What about you? If you could go anywhere in the world, where would it be?"

"New York City! I want to see the lady." Padma held her arm up in the air.

"The Statue of Liberty?" I asked.

"Yes! I've always wanted to see her!" Her eyes widened, and she tipped her head back as if she could see it already. "I told my father once when I was little that I wanted to go there, to see the green statue. He slapped my face and said all I would ever see is the inside of my husband's home, said that was all I was fit for." She held herself together for a few seconds before she crumbled and the tears started.

I got the feeling that when Padma had these moments of remembering her abuse, it wasn't simply that single instance filling her head, but dozens and dozens of them piling on her until she cracked under the weight of them. It was troubling to say the least.

"I thought you said I would forget. Why is he still here?" Padma demanded.

"It will go," Miaka promised, hugging her new sister. "But if you hold on, it can stay longer than you want. You have to let it go."

I motioned to Elizabeth. "That's why she remembered more than any of us. And Aisling had things she held close to her as well."

"Really?" Miaka asked.

"Yes. She kept most of it to herself, but there were huge pieces of her past life that stayed." I placed my hand on Padma's. "We understand that your father's abuse was a big part of your life. That's why it clings to you so terribly. But if you let it stop mattering, that will help."

"Do you think I want this to matter?" she yelled, ripping herself away from us and shoving the chair to the floor in the process. Padma stared us all down for a moment before turning away. "Here I am, beautiful, immortal . . . and all I can think about is that he gets away with killing me. He'll never suffer for what he's done. It's so unfair."

"It is terribly unfair," Elizabeth said fiercely, grasping Padma's hand. "But all you can do now is rejoice in your new freedom. He can never hurt you again. He has no power over you."

New York City was a terrible idea. Yes, there was plenty of water around, but it wasn't exactly easy to get to without being seen. And even in the safety of an apartment, the walls might not be thick enough to hold our voices in, to protect the people around us. And yet, if it would ease some of Padma's pain . . .

"Padma," I began. "You can prove your father wrong on at least one point. Do you want to go live in New York for a while?"

She turned back to us. "Really?"

Elizabeth smiled. "Of course. New sister gets to pick the new town. It's kind of a rule," she lied.

Padma covered her mouth with her hands, completely in shock. "You're not joking with me, are you?"

"Not at all." Miaka opened her laptop. "I'll see if I can find us a nice apartment close to the water."

"Don't be afraid to look outside of Manhattan," Elizabeth said. "We can still go into the city, like, all the time."

"Any level of privacy would be nice. We don't want to have to be rude to the neighbors so they don't bother us," I said. "And we'll have to be very careful that no one hears us."

"Can we find one where I can actually see the Statue of Liberty every night?"

"Guys!" Miaka said, placing her arms up in front of her and giving us a cocky grin. "A little bit of trust, please? I will find us a wonderful home."

Padma squealed and spun around and around, temporarily forgetting all her past hurts. Within the next two days, depending on where the Ocean found a ship, we would head off to sing. I hoped that the promise of this new adventure would outweigh the sorrow of her first song and of the life I wished she would put behind her.

Don't look at their faces, I encouraged Padma as we made our way to the spot the Ocean had selected. *Some will cry out, and that's hard to ignore, but try your best just to focus on the song.*

Padma shook her head. *But I don't know the song.*

It just comes, Miaka explained. *She'll tell you when to start, and all you have to do is obey.*

I can do that, she said. *Just sing?*

I nodded. *Just sing.*

The water was lush and warm as we slowed, and Elizabeth led the way, walking up to the surface. The location alone gave away Her desperation. There was no storm to call a ship into, nor rocks to crash it on. There was nothing but a beautiful tropical shading of clouds and the long line of the horizon in whichever direction we looked. Save the lone silhouette in the distance of the ship that would meet us shortly.

Elizabeth turned to Padma. "You all right?"

"I'm scared. I don't want to kill people."

Miaka came closer to her. "None of us want to. I don't think the Ocean even does. But that's how it works: a fraction of lives sustain all the others. It's hard to see the other side of it because you don't face it as closely, but when we get to New York and you walk down the streets for the first time?"

Padma grinned, and everything in her demeanor said she still couldn't believe it was real.

Miaka smiled back at her. "Just remember that all the people you pass get to live that day because of the sacrifice you're making right now. Both yours and theirs," she said, flicking her head toward the boat.

Padma nodded. "I understand. I'm ready."

We took our places. I lay across the water, the way Aisling had liked to do. Miaka knelt behind me, fanning out her dress.

"You stay with me," Elizabeth said, holding on to Padma's hand. "It's okay to feel anxious. Just squeeze my hand, and I'll be here."

"Okay."

I smiled up at Elizabeth, who was too busy looking at

Padma to notice. I was sure her wild side was still there, that it had been hibernating on Pawleys Island and would roar to life in New York. But it was plain to see the good that Padma brought out in her.

How are you feeling today? the Ocean whispered to me.

Nervous as usual, I admitted. *I'm trying to think about what will come next instead of focusing on what's happening now.*

Keep trying.

I am.

But already I wondered which voice or face would haunt my dreams, mixing in with the other ghosts that seemed to follow me.

Sing.

I didn't have to look back at Padma. She was safe in Elizabeth's care. As always, the song filled us and spilled into the empty sky, as if we poured tea into a waiting cup, warm and fluid. I watched as the boat deviated from its course, searching for the sound. A few moments later, I was sure whoever was at the helm had spotted the unbelievable mirage. *Four girls!* they'd be gasping. *Four girls singing on the water!*

Out of nowhere, a massive bubble erupted from beneath the water, breaking the surface tension and causing the ship to tilt heavily to one side. There was a single roar of screaming. I plugged my ears and kept singing, trying to speed up the process.

It wasn't until the boat was nearly on top of us, listing strangely to the right, that this singing turned into a new kind of nightmare.

This wasn't a fishing boat or a ferry. There was a slide on the deck into a pool that was slowly pouring its contents over the side. A rock wall, a movie screen . . . it was a huge cruise ship. When I focused on the water in front of me, there were so many faces.

And they were dressed so elegantly. A young woman in a blue satin gown slid silently beneath the waves, a look of blissful concentration on her face as she listened to our song. Beside her, a man in a tuxedo dived deep and never resurfaced. All around us, people plunged into the water, their fine dresses and slacks seeming grotesque against the backdrop of so much death.

But with all that, I didn't realize it was a wedding until I caught sight of the bride.

A long white veil floated around her, and her lacy dress was already sodden and heavy with water. Her eyes were fixed on mine, blankly peaceful under the influence of our song. I was sure that she had thought this would be the happiest day of her life, not the last. It was impossible to tell which of the tuxedoed men around her was her groom; perhaps he had already been swallowed by the waters.

Suddenly, I felt nauseated. This bride had found her love, like I had. But there wouldn't be a happy ending for either of us. Shaken, I stopped singing.

Even though my sisters continued, my silence brought awareness back into the bride's eyes, and she began to flounder in the water. "Michael!" she called, staring around frantically. "Michael?" She looked at me again, her eyes pleading with mine. I wanted to look away, but I felt like I owed her, as if watching her die dignified it. Tears spilled down my face.

"Please," she said, still staring into my eyes. Her voice was quiet, but it carried across the water, over the voices of my still-singing sisters.

Mindlessly, I stood and started to walk across the water toward her, clueless as to what I'd do when I got there.

Before I could go far, Elizabeth ran up, flattening me on the water. She gripped my hair, turning my face toward hers, and she sang on, all the while staring daggers at me.

I thrashed against her arms. "Get off me!"

Sing. The Ocean's voice was stern and urgent.

Elizabeth yanked me back to my feet.

"Sing!" she insisted, stopping her own song. Behind her, Miaka's and Padma's voices carried on. "Can't you see you're making it worse? Sing. End it!"

I looked over at the victims of our unfortunate beauty. A few of the wedding guests were coming to their senses in the absence of my and Elizabeth's voices.

"Please, Kahlen. You're putting us all in danger."

I begged the Ocean instead. "Save her! There's room for one more!"

No wives. No mothers. Would you sentence her to this life? I could hear the sorrow in Her voice.

I stopped. No. A century of murder was far crueler than a few moments of fear.

I cradled my head over Elizabeth's shoulder and began the song again, Elizabeth's voice weaving with mine. I couldn't bear to watch the people suffering, so instead I focused on Miaka and Padma. There were too many emotions in their faces to read: sympathy, disappointment, anger, distrust.

We sang until the last scream quieted, until the ship was resting on the Ocean floor. The silence afterward was razor sharp, far more painful than the screams I'd just endured.

Miaka, angrier than I had ever seen her, grabbed me and shook me by the shoulders. "She could have killed you! She's done it for much less! How could you do that to yourself? To us?"

This wasn't what I'd been expecting. They were supposed to understand. They were the only ones who could.

I closed my eyes. "I'm so weary of death."

"We're all tired of death," Elizabeth said, the harshness of her voice shocking me. Tears were running down her face—a thing that never happened—and I was riddled with shame knowing it was because of me. Padma, too, was emotional. Probably for her own reasons, and another layer of guilt hit me for adding confusion to her very first sinking. Elizabeth tugged on my arm, bringing back my focus. "But your service to Her is almost finished, so do your job."

I waited for the Ocean to respond, to tell Elizabeth that, yes, I'd made a mistake, but at least no one lived to tell the tale. Our singing had been successful. But She didn't.

I'd never been more alone.

I ran and dived, pushing myself up the coast.

I'm sorry.

It doesn't matter, I shot back.

Don't isolate yourself right now. It won't help things.

I sped up, moving as quickly as I could without Her help. *I can't stand to be with them. I don't even want to be with myself. I've spend so much time talking myself out of the possibility that I'm evil. But it's true. It's the truest thing I know.* I was aching. I'd given up so much, and seeing the drowning bride had brought it all home to me.

I couldn't be in love. I murdered love every time I sang.

No. You're not evil. You have the softest heart I've ever held. If anything, I'm evil for making you carry this burden.

I blinked back tears and clenched my jaw tightly, hot with anger. *You know what? You're right. You are evil. You've taken everything from me. I have no family, no life. I don't even have hope anymore. You killed everything good in me, and I hate You for it.*

The usually comforting warmth of Her embrace felt colder now, as if She was flinching away from me.

I'm sorry. For all of it. I'm so sorry.

Get the hell out of my head!

I drove myself to the shore, seeing the glow of a lighthouse and using it as my guide to land. I crawled up onto a rocky coast in the fresh darkness of evening. I pulled myself away from the Ocean and onto the grass, clutching my knees to my chest, so worn-out. I couldn't forget the desperate, pleading look on the bride's face. How many more times would I have to do this?

It had been such a long life. I didn't know how much more I could bear, how many more lives I could be responsible for extinguishing. I couldn't forget the faces of the people I'd killed, and I didn't think I could face another twenty years of death. I'd done my best to come to terms with who I was, but never, not once, had I been at perfect peace with myself.

What was I supposed to do now? Maybe I should just ask the Ocean to end my life. My heart was dying. Maybe my body should as well.

I shook my head, ashamed at the thought. What would another death do?

There had to be more than this.

"Kahlen?"

There were things I thought I might remember if I had a second chance at them. Like, if I could hug my mother again, I hoped that, after everything, I'd be able to recognize her embrace among a hundred others. Here it was, as familiar as if I'd lived with it every day, a voice that nothing but the end of my sentence had a chance of erasing from my memory.

I turned to the voice, wondering if I was the fairy tale right now, or if he was.

14

I hadn't given any conscious thought to where I was going, but somehow my headlong rush away from my sisters, away from my guilt, had brought me here. Port Clyde, on the coast of Maine. The place where I had longed to be, where it had seemed impossible that I could end up.

Akinli emerged from the shadows of the lighthouse, examining me with shock in his weary eyes. It had only been about six months since I'd seen him, but he'd changed so much. His scraggly hair was now just a few inches above his shoulders, and he had a hint of a shadow across his chin. His khaki pants had been traded for tattered jeans, and his eyes carried a sadness nearly as heavy as mine.

"Are you all right?"

Should I be asking you the same thing?

I shook my head. I'd never been worse.

Dumbfounded, he knelt in front of me as if trying to make sense of my presence. He ran his hands over my arms, checking for injuries. Even as miserable as I was, his concern for me made me feel infinitesimally better. "You're drenched. Did you fall off a boat or something? Please tell me you didn't go for a swim in a prom dress."

I shook my head again.

"You don't look like you're bleeding. Do you think you have any broken bones?"

No.

"How are you even here? I'm so confused, I . . ." He continued to stare. "I don't even know what to ask next. I . . . Do you have anywhere to go?"

No.

He poked his fingers into the grass, fidgeting, deciding. "Okay then, come with me." Akinli rose and held out a hand.

I stared at his uncut nails, the dirt still clinging to him. I should not be near this boy. I'd just committed an act so unspeakable that if I could use my voice, I'd cry for days. I was isolated from my sisters, estranged from the Ocean. I was so, so deadly.

But what else could I do? Brush him off and say I was

fine when I clearly had been through something? Hop into the water, though I couldn't stand to be near Her right now?

I could stay for a night. Once I was settled, I would come up with a plan. So I slipped my cold hand into his and let him guide me home.

I studied Akinli as we walked. His hand was on my back, leading me to his house, and his palm felt rough and callous, a sign that he was no longer handling books but something much sturdier. He seemed weathered, less buoyant. Why was he still here? He should have been at school.

"It's nice out tonight. You couldn't pick a better evening to go and get yourself lost. I mean, look at that moon. Perfect night for getting lost, don't you think?"

I couldn't help but smile. It was as if we hadn't missed a beat, as if I hadn't left him so coldly and vanished without a word.

"I've thought about you a lot," he continued without looking at me. "When you disappeared, I was really worried." He swallowed. "I tried to find you, but all I had was a first name. The school had no record of anyone going by Kahlen enrolled as a student, and I couldn't find you online. It was almost like you'd never existed at all. Yet here you are."

Panic ran through me, my chest tightening. How was I supposed to explain without creating a pit of lies I'd inevitably fall into? I breathed deeply, trying not to lose it. Should I just run? If I disappeared again, I could make sure he never found me.

He looked me over. What was he thinking? What was he guessing? Undoubtedly, the truth was too far-fetched for him to imagine. But I sensed he was trying to put all the pieces of my story together and none of them fit.

He finally spoke again, quiet and a little wistful. "I kept hoping you'd come back to the library."

I dropped my eyes and put my hands together in a pleading gesture, trying to make him see how sorry I was, that I hadn't wanted to hurt him.

"It's okay," he said, his voice brightening. "I wasn't mad. I was worried. It's just nice to know you're not hurt. Well . . . I hope you're not. Come on."

He turned us toward a two-story house covered in pale-blue paint with black shutters. It looked like his only neighbors had settled in for the night, the light of their TV flickering against the curtains. On the other side of his house, the land turned and the road followed. I could hear the sound of waves crashing nearby.

"I was sad not to have you around, but I don't blame you for disappearing. I disappeared myself not too long after."

I watched him, confused. What could have happened? We walked up the steps and across the porch, and he drew his hand across his face, as if to wipe away his sorrow.

"Julie?" he called, opening the door. "Put on some coffee. We've got company. Julie's my cousin's wife," he told me. "She was a volunteer EMT in college, so you're in good hands."

The front room of the house was the kitchen, and I wasn't sure who Julie was expecting to see when she rounded in from the living room, but she stopped dead in her tracks when she came upon me.

"Uh. Hi." She looked at Akinli. "Who's this?"

"Kahlen. I know her from school, and I found her washed up on the shore by the lighthouse. She, uh, she doesn't talk."

Julie pointed at my gown. "You found her like that?"

"Yeah."

Her training came out in an instant, and she began feeling my arms and looking at my pupils. "She's freezing. She might be in shock. I'll run up and get her some blankets. Ben! Come here!" she called as she raced up the steps.

Akinli moved me to a worn chair in the living room. He pulled open a cupboard and threw a quilt over me, then went back into the kitchen and fumbled around in a drawer, returning with a pen and paper.

"Here. Can you tell me what happened?"

I gaped at the paper, wondering if an answer might magically appear for me. Finally, I wrote: *I don't know.*

"Don't know or don't know how to say?"

I wiggled my hand in front of him, a fifty-fifty gesture.

"Okay. Is there anyone I should call? Family, friends?"

I shook my head.

"No one?"

I looked down at my hands. I'd gotten myself into a very tricky situation here. How could I explain that no one was looking for me because my only family was a bunch of slightly mythological girls and they knew I couldn't get myself into much more trouble than I was already in?

Just then Julie returned with Ben. I recognized him immediately from the pictures in Akinli's dorm room. He had the same chin and the same eyes, and he used them to look me over, wearing a confused expression as comical as his wife's.

"Dude, what the hell?" he said to Akinli.

"I didn't do anything! I just found her. I'm trying to figure out how to get her home, but she doesn't seem to remember much. And she's mute, so it's a little complicated."

Julie put her hand on Ben's shoulder. "Maybe we should call the police. I'm sure someone's looking for her."

I shook my head hard, tapped the paper to get their

attention, and wrote, *Don't bother the police. I'm okay.*

I stared pleadingly at Julie, understanding that she was acting as a mother in this house. Luckily, her eyes widened in sympathy. "What can we do to help you?" she asked. "If we can't call the police, can we take you somewhere? A hospital?"

I'll be fine, I wrote. *I'm just stranded at the moment.*

I clasped my hands in front of me, thinking, as Julie read what I'd written. I knew what I wanted, but I didn't know how to ask. Akinli scooted around, reading my note over Julie's shoulder.

"What if she stayed here with us?" Akinli asked. Julie looked up at him, startled, and Ben frowned.

"I'm not sure that's a good idea," he said in a whisper, as if my muteness also made me deaf. "I'm not comfortable with a stranger in the house."

"But she's not a stranger," Akinli said. "I told Julie. We know each other from school. Look, I even—" He pulled out his phone, fumbling with buttons. "See, that's her."

I'd almost forgotten about the one picture I'd sent him, snuggled and half hidden in my bed.

Ben made a face, agreeing that I was in fact the same girl. While he was clearly still skeptical, Julie seemed mollified.

"Are you sure you'll be okay here?" she asked me. "Don't you have somewhere to be?"

This all felt incredibly awkward, inviting myself into

their home. But I didn't see another option at this point. I couldn't just walk out into the night as if nothing had happened, and I couldn't let them hand me over to a police officer or a paramedic.

And it was highly unlikely that I'd ever get to spend a night under the same roof as Akinli ever again.

I shook my head and wrote, *I'd like to stay, if you didn't mind. Just for a night.*

She frowned worriedly, clearly still concerned, but nodded. "If that's all we can do for you."

I still felt tender and fragile, haunted by what I'd done, but I looked at Akinli and smiled.

After some debate over where to put me, Julie decided I should sleep in the spare room, and she set about making up the sofa bed, then brought me a pair of pajamas. I was grateful for something to wear that wasn't made of Ocean, despite them looking a little too big.

"There are more blankets in this closet if you need them. Even though it's spring, it can get cold up this far north. Not sure if you're from Florida or not, so, uh, yeah."

Julie stammered, filling the uncomfortable space with words.

"Also, I put a cup and a new toothbrush in the downstairs bathroom for you. If you think of anything you need, just let someone know."

I nodded, grateful for her kindness. The true gift she gave me was time, but that she thought of a dozen other niceties made me feel incredibly fond of her. She nodded and then placed her hands on her hips.

"This is a bit weird, isn't it?" she asked, gesturing to us and the room.

I grimaced and nodded.

"Well, weirdness aside, you can stay here as long as you need. Any friend of Akinli's is a friend of ours. Haven't seen too many of 'em lately," she admitted sadly. "So you're a welcome change."

Julie smiled, and I had a feeling that she and I were on the same side, for at least the time being, and that made me like her even more.

"I'll let you get ready for bed. Good night."

When she closed the door, I looked out the wide window that faced the Ocean. She was calling out to me. *Where are you? Are you all right?*

I rolled my eyes. It wasn't as if I could die. She knew that. So I ignored Her and slipped into Julie's pajamas, pausing to roll up the legs.

I emerged from the room to find Akinli on the couch, in pajamas of his own. I was so happy to see him waiting for me.

"Hey," he said, standing. "We've got food if you want."

I signed *no*, forgetting he didn't know sign language.

But he remembered the gesture from our one date and continued.

"Okay. Do you want to watch some TV? If you're tired, you can just go to bed, but I was going to sit here for a while."

In the light of the lamp, I noticed the shadows under Akinli's eyes. He looked much older and more experienced than he had six months ago, but the same warm acceptance shone in his gaze.

I couldn't stay, I reminded myself. I would have to leave tomorrow, go back to my sisters. I could only allow myself one day with him. I didn't want to go to bed; I wanted to spend every ordinary moment I could with Akinli. Maybe I could pretend, just for tonight.

I nodded, and we settled onto the couch together. I pulled into a ball to cover myself up; I felt so insecure in Julie's clothes. Akinli mistook this posture for coldness and pulled a blanket off the back of the couch and messily spread it over me. He hardly even acknowledged that he'd done it, just swept it down and picked up the remote again, making the volume louder.

The channel was clearly sports focused, and the current game featured giant men in tight clothes.

Akinli noticed my puzzled expression and laughed.

"It's a strong-man competition. These things crack me up."

We watched as men carried refrigerators, lifted huge boulders, and flipped massive tires in strange races. I watched, slack jawed, as the competitions got more and more bizarre. By the time the first man came up to pull an eighteen-wheeler into motion from a standstill, I was pointing at the screen, shaking my fingers wildly. I couldn't believe any human was that strong!

"I know, I know!" he cried out. "It's crazy!"

I nodded, a giddy smile on my face. Watching TV had never felt so normal.

After a few contests, he lowered the sound. He seemed nervous, flicking his eyes between the television and me as he started his questions.

"Have you been okay? Since October?"

He handed the pen and paper back to me, but this was one of those things that was beyond words.

I wobbled my head back and forth, trying to say a little yes and a little no.

"I got nervous when you just turned into a ghost." He flicked his fingers open as if I were a flash of smoke.

Again, there was nothing I could say to this. Akinli fidgeted in his seat, finally pushing himself to where he was mostly facing me.

"Okay, I realize that you're kind of stuck here tonight, so maybe it's unfair to ask, but I just have to know. Did I do something wrong?"

I shook my head adamantly.

"Are you sure? Because I thought we were having a great night, and then you were gone, and I have played that date over and over in my head trying to figure out what I did."

I sighed, setting the pad straight in my hand. The pen hung for a long time as I considered my words.

It definitely wasn't you.

He squinted. "Did someone else that night bother you? I know they were a crazy bunch, but—"

I shook my head again, pointing the pen at my chest.

"So, what, you just had to go?"

I nodded, a little embarrassed.

He squinted. "So it was you? You alone? No one else made you go?"

I swallowed. The Ocean's rules were the catalyst, and Her deeply possessive nature was in the back of my mind, but it had been my idea. Right?

After some consideration, he pursed his lips as if he was storing this information.

"You know, there's something else," he said solemnly. "You never told me your favorite color before you left."

I grinned and shook my head at this ridiculous boy. *So many, but mostly I like the color of autumn.*

"The color of autumn," he repeated slowly. "Yeah, how everything looks like it's on fire."

But it's dying! Death never looked so lovely.

He chuckled. "Excellent point. I like a good blue myself. Maybe 'cause I grew up on the water. What else? Uh, favorite food?"

I made a face. *Cake, obviously.*

"Oh, I can't believe I missed that! And by the way, a few months ago I was in a store and saw how expensive almond extract was. We should have been charging per slice. Yikes!"

Nah! I was happy to share.

"Well maybe we should have been less eager. I got harassed for more treats up until the day I left. Seriously. So, just so you know, you broke the heart of the entire second floor in Jabbison Hall when you left. They were crushed over the loss of cake." I appreciated Akinli's teasing. I had been afraid that he'd be mad or bitter. Knowing that he'd mostly been worried made being back beside him so easy. Too easy.

"Oh, here's a good one. I think this says a lot about a person. Favorite smell?"

I considered for a moment.

"I'll go first, if you like. I love the smell of fresh-cut grass." I gave him a thumbs-up, because that was a good one. "I heard that the smell is actually the grass trying to say it's in distress, which makes me a little sad about it, but it's still really good."

155

I took up my pad. *So what does that say about you? Enjoys the outdoors? Yearns for freedom? Willingly mows lawns?*

He laughed. "All of the above. What about you?"

I flipped to the next page. It wasn't until I started writing it down that I realized the memory had even stayed with me. It was like a special gift after all this time.

Any flowers. My mother used to like to have fresh flowers in the house.

"So, not even specific, just any flower at all?"

I nodded.

Akinli's smile faded as he read over the page again. "Wait a minute. 'Used to'? She doesn't anymore?"

I closed my eyes, realizing I'd been thoughtless. I hadn't intended to let him know that.

"Is your mom gone?"

Looking down at my hands so I wouldn't be drawn to lie, I nodded.

"Your dad?"

I nodded again.

"How?" he breathed, as if he was almost afraid to ask.

I felt numb for a minute, recalling the carpet, and my mother watching herself in a mirror as the boat heaved.

They drowned. I'd said the words before, but I'd never written them down. It was much harder to face in print.

I preferred to think of it as an accident, though the images of murder at the Ocean's hands or suicide at their own were the ones that tried to force their way to the front.

He let out a breathy sound, almost like a laugh. "That's crazy."

There was a long pause as he sat there, staring at anything in the room but me.

"A few weeks after you left, I got a call from my mom. Which, you know, was no surprise, because she called me every day. But even from her saying hello . . . I knew something was wrong." He paused to swallow and started toying with a thread on the couch. "She had cancer. It was pretty serious, and I wanted to go home right away. They wanted me to finish the year, so we compromised, and I went home at Christmas break.

"Dad was adamant that I was going back to school. I wasn't sure I could, even after whatever happened with Mom. I didn't want to leave him alone, you know?" He looked up at me, and I gave a tiny nod. I did. I understood what it meant to stay.

"I was supposed to be with them," he said. It was all he could get out before looking away again. He tried not to make a big deal of wiping away the tears in his eyes. "Mom had a doctor's appointment, and Dad was taking her. I was going to go, too, but Mom . . . I'll never forget it. She told me to stay. Every time I tried to argue about it, she insisted I stay. Sometimes I wonder if she knew."

He stared at nothing, haunted.

"It was rainy," he continued. "The roads here can flood sometimes if it gets bad. The police weren't sure if my dad saw a deer or just hit a bad patch, but he swerved right into a tree."

I covered my mouth, eyes brimming.

"I'd been bracing myself for Mom, but losing them both at once . . . I wasn't ready for that."

I crawled across the couch, sitting next to him, scribbling on the pad.

I should have been with mine, too.

He squinted. "Did you nearly drown?"

I nodded.

He sighed. "Looks like you nearly drowned again tonight." He wiped at a tear in the corner of my eye. "Seems like water isn't your friend."

I tried to control my face, not wanting to give away that water was so much more and so much less than that.

We were getting into dangerous territory here, a place where I couldn't keep my secrets. And Akinli looked incredibly tired, and I felt guilty keeping him up any later. So I pointed to the clock, to myself, and then to my room, letting him off the hook.

"Yeah, you're probably right." Though he seemed as hesitant to part ways as I was.

I crossed to the guest room, hearing Akinli stand as I reached the door.

"Will you be okay alone? I could sit with you if you want. I know it's been a crazy night."

He brushed his too-long hair out of his face, and I stared into his beautiful blue eyes. It had been hard enough to talk myself out of liking him six months ago. But now, seeing him so typical, so at home, so very human . . . it was almost impossible to think about walking out the door tomorrow.

But, of course, I'd have to. And eventually, I'd have to go back to the Ocean. I still owed Her nineteen years. Who would he be in nineteen years? A husband? A father? And what would I be? A teenage girl who'd spent the last century killing and running, now penniless, nameless, and pointless.

I signed *no*, snapping my fingers together, and it was a relief that there was one word between the two of us that needed no translation.

"Okay. Well, I'll be out here if you need me."

I nodded.

"And hey," he added quickly, shoving his hands into the pockets of his sweatpants. "Even though the circumstances are weird, it's nice to see you again."

I smiled as I turned and went into the room.

Without Akinli's jokes and laughs to distract me, I could once again hear the Ocean calling for my return. Just a few hundred feet from the water, I was too far away for Her to find me.

Where are you? Your sisters are worried. Come back. Kahlen, come back.

I lay on my bed, listening to Her go on and on. The anxious tone implied Her wringing Her hands and pacing, like a mother who'd lost her child in a crowd.

Well, maybe now She could understand how all the friends and relatives of the people She'd devoured over the years had felt. Besides, She was being dramatic. Where could I go? It wasn't as if I could die without Her help.

Come back. Where have you gone? Why aren't you answering?

She pleaded endlessly with me. I would. Of course I would. What else could I do?

I heard the door to the spare room creak and pretended to be asleep, hoping I could pull off looking like a normal person for just a few more hours.

I felt a warm hand touch my forehead. And then my cheek. I held my act steady though Akinli's touch made me feel more than awake.

"Where in the world did you come from, you beautiful, silent girl?" he whispered. After a long moment, I heard him slowly creep out of the room, quietly closing the door behind him.

I pressed my lips together, wanting to cry. He'd touched me before in passing, but that brush against my cheek was so incredibly tender, it was almost impossible to take.

In my first life, I'd never crossed paths with anyone I wanted to be with, and I had no promise that I would once my sentence was up. So why, here and now, in this frozen, useless time, did someone have to make me feel this way?

I couldn't keep him. And I couldn't even be sure how deep his feelings went, though I sensed he was as curious about me as I was about him. This was bound to be a disaster.

I couldn't stay forever.

But at least I could stay for a day.

15

When the sun came up, I was still awake, thinking of Akinli's callous fingers on my cheek. I heard the others waking and moving around in the kitchen. I sat up, staring out the window. The Ocean continued Her cries, but I wasn't ready to face Her yet. Or to leave Akinli.

"So I'll be on the boat till the afternoon, and I need to talk to Evan." Ben was talking with his mouth full.

"I'll go out tomorrow," Akinli promised. "I mean, we've been hitting our numbers."

"It's no big deal. I know you're *indisposed* today."

I smirked to myself. For one day, Akinli belonged to me.

The noise settled down, doors opened and closed, cars

came and went. After a while, all I could hear was Akinli lumbering around in the kitchen.

About eight he knocked on the door and poked his head in. I was already sitting up, and he smiled in greeting.

"Good morning, prom queen." I looked across the room at the dress. I'd need to get rid of that before it fell apart.

He came in with two plates of food and sat on the bed with me while we ate. The meal tasted completely average, which led me to believe he'd made it. With his history of disastrous cooking, I appreciated the effort.

"So Ben and Julie are gone for most of the day. Do you want to do a little sightseeing, or is there somewhere you need to go?"

I shook my head.

"This is a really pretty area, totally different from Miami. I remember you saying you grew up kind of all over the place, but have you ever been to Maine?"

I thought back. No.

"So, I've decided that we're going to have the best day. Nothing bad is allowed to happen, and if it does, we'll find the bright side. I think we both deserve a good day, don't you?"

I nodded.

"Good. I really wanted to thank you for listening to me talk about my parents last night. Ben is like a brother to me, and Julie, well . . ."

I widened my eyes and brought up my hands.

"Yeah, she's the best. I'm really glad they took me in, but, I don't know, sometimes it's hard to talk to them."

I nudged him with my elbow, hoping he knew I didn't mind being his sounding board in the slightest.

"And thanks for sharing about your family, too. I know it's not easy to talk about."

I shrugged. It was too complicated to explain that I missed them and yet could barely remember them.

"This might sound weird, but right after we met, I did some research. I thought it was kind of fascinating that you could hear but not speak. I found out that people who aren't deaf are usually mute for one of two reasons. Either it's a physical thing, like a deformed tongue or something, or it's because something happened, and emotionally they can't speak anymore. I wondered . . ."

I held up a number two. It hurt so much to speak. To sing. To laugh. My voice was death, and I hated it.

"Okay. Well, then I'll cross my fingers that one day it'll be possible for you again. I have this feeling you have enough thoughts to fill books. And I'd love to hear them."

His eyes were soft, and that safe feeling that surrounded him enveloped me. There was a look of wonder on his face as he watched me, and, despite our mutual sorrow, I smiled at him.

16

Julie had left me a pair of jeans, a T-shirt, and a cardigan. As I rinsed my mouth out in the bathroom and brought my gaze up to the mirror, I took a good look at myself. My hair had those loose, beachy waves in it that some girls tried to create artificially, and my eyes were bright, full of expectation. Something about being a siren seemed to accentuate the best of our features, but today I thought I was pretty, just on my own. I felt young and perfectly, wonderfully normal.

I galloped down the stairs and found Akinli sitting in front of the TV, ready to go in his own set of jeans and a cotton shirt. I noticed he'd also shaved and pulled his long hair up into a little bun.

"Okay," he announced. "You want to get out for a bit? I've got the truck." He waved the keys in the air.

I nodded enthusiastically. It was barely nine in the morning. We had a whole day to play.

"We're still unsure of the cause," a newscaster replied on-screen. "We might be looking at another mystery of the Bermuda Triangle here."

I couldn't turn away from the images of debris floating on the water, deck chairs and loose clothes and flowers.

"Rescue workers are still hoping to find survivors, but currently, no one is here to give any insight as to what caused the sinking. According to reports, the ship veered off course, going several miles in a direct line to this spot, before suddenly capsizing. But the weather was clear, and there are no records of a distress signal coming from the captain or crew, so the reason for the sinking is truly a mystery. We're getting reports of family members posting images of missing passengers online, but easily the most heartbreaking story from this is the loss of Karen and Michael Samuels, who had been married only hours before. Our thoughts are with them and their families and close friends, all of whom were lost in the sinking."

I grabbed the remote out of Akinli's grasp, smashing buttons, trying to cut it off.

"Hey, hey, hey," he said, taking hold of my hands. I gripped the remote as he aimed it and flicked off the TV, holding on to me the whole time.

My breathing was ragged. Typically, I would have called that information useful, something I could write in my scrapbook. But seeing a picture of Karen and Michael kissing with their cheering friends behind them, lives lost because they wanted to support them, was too much.

"You okay?"

I swallowed.

He stared at me as I gazed at the dark television.

"I have a hard time watching the news sometimes, too. There's too much bad in the world."

I nodded.

"But, you know what, that didn't even happen today. It happened yesterday. And today is going to be the best day, remember?"

I let the tension out of my body, the remote falling out of my grip and into Akinli's. He was right. It was only one day, and I couldn't have it ever again. For once, I had to shrug off the sadness. I couldn't change what had happened, but I could choose to enjoy today.

I signed my thanks.

"Umm, you're welcome?" he guessed.

And I smiled, nodding, grateful for his presence.

"Come on, prom queen. You can't have the best day ever unless you get in the best truck ever."

Always the gentleman, he walked me to the passenger's

side and opened the door for me. April in the south meant getting ready for shorts, but here, the cold hand of winter still pinched at the air. With the windows cracked, we got a wonderful breeze as we headed around town.

"Hey, Ms. Jenkens," Akinli called as we drove past an older woman sitting on her porch. He greeted or waved to nearly everyone whose path we crossed, seeming to be friendly with the entirety of his small town, and that energy helped lift my mood. I took in the scenery with a fresh sense of awe. We had spent so much time in big cities over the years, and I wasn't used to overgrown lawns or the stretches of empty land that led down to the shore. The paint colors on all the houses were muted, and I wasn't sure if that was by choice or if the sun had worn them down over time.

"Any of this look familiar?" he asked as we drove on a long, gently winding road. "Anything that could help you remember exactly how you got here?"

We passed a church, and houses with metal lawn art. Boats were stuck in sandbars, waiting for high tide to come and rescue them. I noted several signs for lobster, as if no one knew where to find it.

I shook my head. It was the truth. I hadn't seen a bit of this in my life before.

"You really must have washed up on shore then. This is the only way into Port Clyde. I guess yesterday was a rough day at sea all around."

I shook my head. He had no idea.

He hummed along to the music on the radio, blurting out the occasional lyric, then looking embarrassed. "Never was much of a singer. My mom, she was good."

He raised a finger and pointed to the side of the road. Two small wooden crosses stood next to a tree with bark that was still healing. I thought that if I had to go past the spot of my sinking any time I wanted to go somewhere, my heart would cave in on itself. But he smiled as if this place was a reminder that they'd lived, not that they'd died.

He kissed his pointer and middle fingers twice quickly and blew, a simple hello. And as we passed, his mood stayed cheerful, as if he was carrying them with him.

When we finally got to the end of the road, Akinli took a right, and it looked for a moment like we were going to be on another one of these rural roads. But signs of civilization slowly started cropping up: a fast-food chain, a home improvement store, a gas station with illuminated signs. We drove on and on until the road hooked around, and I saw the Ocean resting against yet another harbor. I could still hear Her calling me, a constant, soft pleading, and I purposefully tried to tune Her out. I would have to go back soon enough. For now, I was following Akinli's lead: today belonged to us.

We parked along the street. I turned to look at Akinli,

and he answered the question in my eyes.

"We're in Rockland. It's the biggest town nearby."

I let myself out of the truck before Akinli could get to my door, but he was by my side quickly.

"It's not much, but it's more than Port Clyde. I thought we could look around."

I signed *yes*, and he did it back.

"That's three I've got now. You might need to give me some lessons at some point."

I nodded. I was up for anything that let us talk.

"So there's a jewelry store, some ice cream—that place doesn't actually open for a few hours, but it's so good. We're totally going there. Umm, books are this way."

I clapped.

"Good choice. Let's go."

It was a weekday, and the streets were mostly empty. I had heard people reminisce about old Main Street charm before, and now I understood the appeal. There was a sense of intimacy here, of predictability. I bet there were festivals and street fairs, Christmas parades down this very road.

I walked dreamily toward the bookstore, only snapping to when my fingers accidentally brushed against Akinli's.

He said nothing but laughed a little. "This is it."

A friendly clerk greeted us as we entered. Unlike the polished, massive bookstores in the city, this one was quaint. A hodgepodge of decorations adorned the walls, making everything feel quirky and personal.

I instantly dragged my fingers across a shelf of book spines, in love with each one already. Books were a safe place, a world apart from my own. No matter what had happened that day, that year, there was always a story in which someone overcame their darkest hour. I wasn't alone.

It wasn't long until I found the highlight of the store: the children's section. There was a tiny house with two pillows inside, the roof itself a bookshelf on one side. Up against it was a small desk with a place for children to leave a letter in a mailbox and take one for themselves, and little plastic cubes with words printed on each side intended for making poetry.

"My queen!" Akinli whispered. "Your palace awaits!" He gestured grandly to the tiny house.

I crawled in, ducking my head to fit. I pulled a handful of discarded books up into my arms while Akinli grabbed the poetry cubes.

We were pressed together in the cramped space, and my whole right side was warmed by his skin. I thumbed through stories about pirates, angry vegetables, and budding ballerinas. Akinli rolled the blocks in his hands, laughing at his options.

He placed four cubes reading "the blue is excellent"

across my lap. I gave a thumbs-up and wrote out "smell this sky."

He inhaled deeply. "That's some good sky." He flipped the cubes over and over. "Do you think kids know what *melodic* means?"

I nodded. Eighty years of watching from the sidelines had given me time to observe that children were smarter than people gave them credit for.

"I've never really thought about how funny words are. Like, we can write them out or speak, but then there are how many languages in the world? And then there's Braille. And sign language. It's kind of remarkable."

I agreed. Words, sounds, communication. My world revolved around these things. That and water.

"You're fluent in sign language, right?"

I nodded.

He pulled back just a little so he could see me. "Tell me a story. Like, with signs. Tell me the truest story you know."

Akinli's face was expectant and happy. I lifted my eyes to the ceiling, thinking. He wouldn't understand any of this. . . .

"I have three sisters. Miaka, Elizabeth, and Padma. The Ocean is my mother, and we're fighting. That's all I know about myself anymore. I'm certain there used to be more, but I've forgotten it. Altogether, I've lived a hundred years.

I hold on to strange things, like the look of the walls on that ship, and completely forget others, like if I used to have a best friend.

"Some days, I don't know what there's left to live for. I try to memorialize the lives I've helped to take, but I'm not sure it does any good. And I try to take care of my sisters, but I don't think that's enough by itself. I don't think anyone could exist for another person for their entire life."

I paused.

"Maybe they could, though. If they found the right person. At this moment, I'm considering living for you. But you'd never, ever know."

I fought to keep a smile on my face. No matter what, I was determined that today was going to be a good day.

"Besides the part where you pointed to me, I didn't understand a thing . . . but that was really beautiful. You make me want to learn." He held up two fingers. "That's the second time you've inspired me."

I squinted, trying to recall what I could have possibly said or done.

"Remember back in Florida when you said I should look into social work? I checked it out. There were tons of things that felt perfect for me. I love kids. I could help kids."

I signed *yes* over and over.

"Intuitive." He pointed at me. "That's what you are."

With that, he started playing with the blocks again as if he was hunting for a specific word. I picked up another book, and we sat there in the happiest silence I'd ever known.

When it was time to leave, we bought the last book I'd been holding, and as we walked toward the ice cream shop, our hands brushed together again.

This time neither of us flinched.

17

I took a big bite of mint chocolate chip ice cream and
closed my eyes appreciatively as the creamy sweetness
spread over my tongue.

"Told you about the ice cream," Akinli said. "I've heard
that people started religions around this stuff."

Besides the lobster, he'd told me the area was also famous
for its ice cream. I could see why.

"This was one of the things I missed most down at
school. This ice cream. Watching sports with Dad was
another. I mean, it should have been something I could
do with anyone, but it always felt more fun with him. My
mom's smell." He shook his head at himself. "It's weird,
all the things that go into that feeling of being home. And

then it's strange to have to change it."

I wanted to scream out that I knew exactly what he meant. How sometimes the things that made home *home* weren't even things you liked. How I was tired of cool skin and salt. How I had seen sisters and cities come and go over the decades, and it made it hard to know how our little family was going to feel any given year. How it made you wary of letting yourself get comfortable in any place for very long.

"What's your home like?" he asked.

I searched my memories, trying to find one place that felt like somewhere I really belonged. For all the time we'd spend in an area, for all the cities we went to, none of them felt like a safe space to fall.

I shrugged and poked my spoon at my ice cream. I remembered so many things, but home wasn't something definable for me.

"It's okay if you don't want to talk about it. One day you'll make new memories, a new home," he said sadly, reassuringly. "We both will."

I didn't want to fall for the sincerity in his voice, that unselfish stare in his eyes that promised he'd make sure to put all the broken pieces of my life back together. It was too hard to fight though, so I didn't.

I watched this unassuming, calming boy, thinking he had no idea how extraordinary he was. *You feel so safe*, I thought.

"So, there are plenty of other shops we can look at, or we can go back to Port Clyde." Akinli checked the time on his phone. "Ben should be nearly done, and Julie only had the one appointment."

I squinted.

"She's a hair and makeup artist. Not tons of clientele in the town, but she's willing to travel, and she's good, so she's usually booked. Today was a wedding, and when there are formals, like homecoming and stuff, she's always busy." He bit the inside of his cheek, making a face. "Sometimes she tries things out on Ben and me."

I smiled, picturing them in eye shadow and blush.

Akinli picked up his phone, swiping his thumb across the screen. "This was some sort of hydrating mask." He showed me a picture of him and Ben with green stuff smeared across their cheeks. Ben had a beer in his hand, and Akinli had a glass of milk. They made faces as they clinked them together in a toast.

I had to cover my mouth to hold in the laugh.

"Let that be a sign of how much I trust you. No one's seen that picture. I'm only keeping it in case I need to blackmail Ben someday."

I drummed my fingers on the table, the rat-a-tat the closest I could come to laughing.

He chuckled at the sound, glanced at the picture again, and shook his head. "They're great. I'd be lost without them."

I placed my hand on his, touched by his humanness, his ability to care despite his pain, and his little hint of a smile that lingered when there wasn't anything to smile about.

Akinli flipped his palm over, wrapping his fingers around mine. He propped up his head with his other arm, staring at me. I took the same pose, studying this impossible boy.

His eyes were so blue. I felt a little breathless staring into them.

Akinli rubbed his thumb across the back of my hand. "Come on, prom queen, let's go home."

He didn't let go of my hand. Not when he threw away his trash, not when he held the door for the elderly couple coming in for a postlunch treat, not when the sidewalk was so crowded I had to duck behind him. I could still hear the Ocean calling me, and I ignored Her.

The drive back to Port Clyde felt long. He didn't turn the radio back on, and he didn't try to speak. It felt as if we were sizing each other up. The more he watched me, the more I sensed he was guessing there was something otherworldly about me. The longer I looked at him, the more I wondered if he could handle being exposed to me, to my realm, for more than these few hours.

We drove past the artists' residency, the tourists pulling into the lone bed-and-breakfast, and sweet Ms. Jenkens, who was still parked on her porch with a pitcher of tea.

When we reached the house, another car and a scooter were also in the driveway, so I guessed the others were there. Akinli put his hands in his pockets, his eyes downcast as we went up the steps and across the porch.

Opening the door, we came upon Ben wrapping his arms around Julie from behind, Julie bent over in laughter.

"One kiss!" he demanded.

"You stink!" she protested, hitting him with a spatula.

"But I love you!"

I wanted to cry at how beautiful that tiny moment was. Couples were like sirens, making their own languages and signs, their own worlds.

Akinli cleared his throat, alerting them to our presence.

"Oh, wow, you look way less terrifying when you aren't sopping wet and dressed like royalty." Ben laughed at himself, gave the now-disarmed Julie a quick kiss on the cheek, and ran upstairs. "Shower. See you guys in a sec."

Julie's gaze followed him affectionately before she sighed and faced us. "You hungry?"

Akinli poked out his belly and rubbed it. "I'm full of ice cream. You?"

I signed *okay*, a gesture that I knew he would understand.

"All right. I'll just finish this up for Ben." She eyed me. "You look way better in my clothes than I do."

"How was it today?" Akinli asked, getting some juice from the fridge.

Julie beamed. "Wonderful. Weddings are the best. Well, except for that one earlier this year," she amended.

Akinli turned to me. "A few months ago, Julie had a bride throw a glass of champagne at her."

I stared wide-eyed at Julie. "I'm still not sure how it happened," she said, chuckling. "I vaguely remember an eyelash curler being involved, but once things started flying, I packed my kit and bolted."

"Nothing like that today?" Akinli spoke to Julie, but his eyes were on me. I tried not to stare back.

"Nope. Positively blissful, and the happy couple should be man and wife by now," she commented, checking the clock. "And Ben had a good morning, too. He also filled the gas in the boat. You," she said, pointing a fork at Akinli, "have got to stop taking it out at night."

He made a face. "What? Come on."

"Those little trips add up."

"Okay, what if I drop traps when I go?"

"If you go."

"Aw, puh-leease," he whined.

Julie laughed, and I sensed she would back down on the debate. Ben would probably be a bit harder to convince.

In the middle of this mundane moment, I found myself close to tears. It was refreshing simply to get a peek into a real family. And this one, broken and pieced back together, was better than anything I could imagine.

Leaving was going to be harder than I thought. For many reasons.

Akinli was staring at me again. I could see, as clear as anything, that he was trying to unravel my secrets. I'm not sure at what point it had turned from suspicion to fact, but he knew something was off.

And yet.

He put an arm around me. "Julie, you up for hire tonight?"

Still smiling, she nodded. "Why do you ask?"

"Kahlen and I decided to have the best day ever, and I think she needs a night out. Could you help her with that?"

She followed Akinli's gaze to me. Whatever she saw in my face, her own reflected only sympathy. "Absolutely."

18

Julie didn't ask Akinli or me to pay for her services. Instead, she sent us to the general store—the only store in town—and had us get groceries for her.

"Hey, Akinli! Who's your friend?" greeted the older man behind the counter.

"Kahlen. Friend from school. She's staying for a while."

A while? I thought. *Do you have any idea how impossible the last nineteen hours have been?*

"Nice to meet you, honey," he said, holding out his hand.

I shook it, noting how his skin felt like thin paper. He'd never been a fisherman, for sure.

"Is the Dip Net rented out tonight?" Akinli asked, picking up a basket.

"Nope."

"Good. Kahlen's going to try some of our best food." Akinli winked at me, and I followed him, waving good-bye to the older man. "Have you ever had lobster?" he asked.

I grimaced. After being a siren, the thought of having seafood kind of felt like eating a very distant relative.

"Please tell me this is a joke."

I gave him an awkward smile.

"Seriously? Kahlen, what am I going to do with you?" he teased, continuing down the aisle, grabbing bread crumbs and soup. "You waltz into town like it's nothing, you're such a chatterbox I can never get a word in edge-wise, and then you confess to the most heinous of crimes!" He shook his head. "Don't tell Ben. He may literally kick you out for that one."

Akinli smiled to himself, dragging his hand down the line of shelves. I did the same, taking in the cool metal. I loved this little store, the feel and smell of it. I wished I could come back to it.

"Ouch!" Akinli jerked back his hand. "Be careful."

When he held it up for inspection, there was a thin slice across two of his fingers. I turned to the shelf, seeing the sharp, broken section that must have cut him.

"How's your hand?" he asked, flicking his head at my palm.

I shook my head, knowing I'd be lacking a cut.

"No, really, is it okay?" He reached over and flipped up my hand. Nothing. Not a mark, not a drop of blood. "Hmm," he said, a smirk coming to his face. "You must have some really thick skin."

He stared into my eyes, knowing I should be bleeding. There was nothing accusatory or frightened in his expression, merely a hint of curiosity.

He sighed. "Sadly, I'm merely a mortal. I should probably get some bandages. Hey, Kurt," he called. "You need to fix this shelf back here."

I gently pulled back my hand, and he walked around the corner looking for the medical supplies. I stood alone for a moment, trying to calm the rapid beating of my heart.

Julie ran her fingers through my hair as we stared into the vanity in her room.

"What shampoo do you use? Your hair is like silk," she proclaimed, envy dripping from her voice.

I kept needing to come up with facial expressions that said things for me. How could I make my cheeks say I didn't remember, my forehead express gratitude? I missed words.

"Okay, first things first: hair and makeup. And the restaurant isn't very fancy, so maybe we'll skip your absolutely breathtaking but slightly over-the-top gown, and you can just steal something else out of my closet."

I smiled as she plugged in a curling iron and opened something that looked like a tackle box. There weren't any lures inside. Instead it was filled with powders and blushes, baby wipes and tubes of mascara.

I couldn't help but gawk at the sheer volume of makeup she owned.

"I know, I know. It really needs to be cleaned out a bit, but, trust me, I've used all of this at least once." She held up palettes next to my cheek, looking for just the right one. It was akin to watching Misha with her paints.

"I want to apologize." She grabbed a brush and started pulling it through my hair. "If we seemed standoffish last night, I'm sorry. It's weird to have someone you don't know in your house."

I nodded enthusiastically. I kept marveling at their kindness in letting me stay.

"But Akinli clearly trusts you, and whatever you've been through, I just want you to know you're safe here."

Our eyes met in the mirror, and I saw nothing but compassion in hers. "Honestly, I wouldn't care if you were a mass murderer."

I hoped she didn't notice the way I tensed at her words.

"Anyone who could make Akinli smile like that . . . and he shaved today. He asked me about cutting his hair." She shook her head as if these were huge things. "I know that's all superficial, but he's had a hard time caring about much since his parents passed. Did you know about that already?"

I nodded.

"Good. I would've felt awful if I'd accidentally been a gossip." She pinned a section of my hair to the side, pulling out small pieces to curl. "I don't know what kind of friendship you two had before, or if it was something more than that, but I feel like he woke up today. I haven't seen him like this in a while."

My lips parted in surprise. Because, really, everything from before had been so brief. A handful of moments that seemed to amount to nothing in hindsight.

But then why had I thought of him so often? Why did he respond to me the way he did?

It was one of those moments, sort of like when I thought of Miaka and Elizabeth befriending each other, when I just had to believe they were meant to meet. In my heart, I wanted to say that Akinli and I were meant to be together, but I pushed the thought away. I was going to find a way to leave by morning. For everyone's sake, I had to.

Akinli pulled out my chair as I looked around the little restaurant, so small I might not have noticed it if he hadn't pointed it out to me. Buoys hung down from the ceiling along the bar, and I could peek into the exposed kitchen. Out the side door, the dock extended into the water, and the sky was turning pink and purple around the shadow of moored boats.

I found myself enamored with Port Clyde. It was small, and there wasn't much to do, but it was bursting with personality. Seeing Akinli here made him new to me. Yes, he should go back to school, and yes, it was probably good for him to have been exposed to a bigger city, but he was like a gear in this tiny town, and I wondered how all the others managed to turn while he was gone.

"Okay," he started. "I can't tell if you hate seafood or if you've never had it before."

I held up a number two.

"So are you feeling brave enough to at least try lobster?" He made a pouty face and batted his eyes.

I smiled. Sure.

"I mean, no pressure. I just think you'd love it."

I closed my menu and held my hands up in surrender, and it felt like a huge accomplishment when I made him laugh.

"Okay then."

While we waited, Akinli brought out the trusty pen and pad from his house. I was going to miss this little thing.

"So, what do you think of my town? Be honest," he said, pointing to the paper. "I want a full report."

It was such a pertinent question that I was starting to wonder if he could read my mind.

He gave me some time to get it all out, reading carefully once I was done.

It's beautiful here. I like how quaint everything feels, how you seem to know everyone's name. There's a sense of peace. Close to perfect.

"Close to perfect? You think?"

I signed an enthusiastic *yes*. Now that I'd been in a place like this, where lives connected and crossed, it was easy to see why all those cities had been wrong for me. Anonymity helped, sure. But if you found the right place, with the right kind of people, it was much better going somewhere you might at least get a nod or a wave as you walked home.

"I'm glad you like it here. Really."

We watched the sky turning darker outside the window, and I kept thinking that any moment I'd need to get out of here. I lacked a plausible story, and I really, *really* didn't want to disappear on him again.

A few minutes later, a bright-red lobster was set in front of me with a slice of lemon and a bowl of melted butter. I gave pause, feeling strange.

You're not a fish, I reminded myself. *You're a girl.*

Using a cracking tool, two forks, and occasionally Akinli's fingers, I managed to get some of the meat out. In the end, I agreed it was worth the work, and he watched me with satisfaction as I licked butter off my fingers and ate every last piece.

I basked in the rhythms of Akinli's voice, the constantly changing expressions that crossed his face as he talked. He told me more about growing up in this small town, working on his cousin's boat, spending a childhood safe in his parents' love.

We split a slice of rich cheesecake, and he took my hand as we left the restaurant.

"One more thing. If you don't mind going on a field trip, that is."

I couldn't imagine adding anything else to this day. I knew in my gut this was the time for me to start making excuses. If I had half a brain, I'd tell him to leave me by the general store and pass on my good-byes to Ben and Julie.

But I went with him all the same.

We drove around the small town in a matter of minutes, heading by the lighthouse, Ben's home, and too many dense forests to count, until finally we stopped in front of a darkened house.

Akinli parked in the empty driveway, sighing as he took out the keys. "Last stop of the night. Come on."

The house wasn't a mansion, but in comparison to all the other houses in Port Clyde, it might as well have been. Two stories, with a wraparound porch and a wide, dormant garden curled along the front steps. Akinli fiddled with his keys until he found the right one, unlocked the door, and led us into an empty space.

The moon was full, but that didn't do much to help us once we got inside. I looked at Akinli, who grinned and pulled a lighter out of his pocket. He lit one candle, then another, then another, and I suddenly remembered that I had no idea where he was while Julie had dolled me up.

I followed him, gazing at his handsome face as the rooms grew brighter, falling in love a little more with every spark. He held one candle in his hand and carried it as he walked.

"My grandpa built this house," he said. "He was a rich old man, so while Dad grew up working on a boat, Mom grew up with a vacation house in Maine." He gestured to the walls around us. "Don't think Grandpa was too thrilled when she came one summer and chose to never leave, but I think I ended up being the peacemaker. He was giddy when I was born and spoiled me rotten till he died." Akinli smiled.

"We held an estate sale after Mom and Dad died. They had some money put aside, but a lot of it went for Mom's medical bills. It hurt too much to keep it all anyway. There's more," he said, nodding his head to the back of the house.

We stepped out onto the porch and walked down the slope, getting uncomfortably close to the shouting Ocean. I tried not to listen to Her words.

"This is one of the few houses that has a beach instead of rocks," he bragged, laughing at his own claim. No, there weren't any jagged boulders sticking out, but his beach was maybe two feet wide. "See the light that way? That's the lighthouse, and if we kept following the curve of the coast, we'd be in town."

He smiled, looking back at me, taking my hand in his. "You like this, too?" He motioned toward his house, and I looked up at it. Even with no one living there, it had life to it, and I couldn't deny the beauty of the craftsmanship. It was then that I felt something trickle across my hand.

When I looked back, Akinli had tilted the candle wax over my fingers.

"Hmm," he said as if he'd seen something he knew he would. His eyes came back to mine. "I think that would have burned most people."

I swallowed. I hadn't reacted to the pain at all.

"Listen, Kahlen. I'm not blind. I don't know what to make of a girl who has no last name, who can't or won't share certain details about her life, who can't speak and doesn't get cut or burned, so I've only got two guesses: either you *are* trouble or you are *in* trouble. My guess is it's the latter."

I bit my lip, trying not to cry. If the Ocean could just stop screaming for a minute, I could think. I wanted to tell him no. I *am* trouble. I am such great trouble to you. But what could I do?

He took my face in his hands. "I'm not a rich man,

191

Kahlen, but I do own this house. Thanks to Ben and Julie, I've been saving to start my life back up, but until you washed up on shore, I wasn't sure there was much of a point to it. If you want to stay here, I won't let anything hurt you. If you want to get out of whatever you've been in, I don't care what it is, we'll all take care of you."

My heart was completely gone, his in an instant. He wasn't sure what was wrong with me and wanted me to stay anyway. He didn't know what danger I was in but was ready to fight it for me.

And who was I? No one, really. Just a girl.

But seeing myself through his eyes . . . I felt like so much more.

So how did I do this? How could I stay?

In less than twenty-four hours, I'd made a few slips, but for Akinli's sake, I could do better. The Ocean and my sisters needn't ever know about him. Aisling had taught me that much. And if he really wanted me here, then he'd certainly understand that I might need to disappear for a few hours once a year, maybe less if I was lucky.

If he cared for me the way he said he did, the way I knew he did, he'd have to travel away with me before his friends or family started asking questions about my abnormalities. But at my core, I believed for the first time that it was feasible.

And then, I really could live for someone. Because,

despite all the silence and death and the inevitability of my life, he would be there to balance it out.

It wasn't fairy-tale perfect, but it was possible.

I nodded. Of course. Of course I would stay.

"Yes?"

I nodded. Yes.

With my face still cupped in Akinli's hands, he kissed me. It was brief, but it was enough to send fireworks running down my veins.

"You have brought me back from the dead," he whispered. He must have noted the dreamy look in my eyes, because almost instantly, he lowered his lips to mine again.

I'd waited an eternity for this. I'd have waited all over again if I had to. I was meant to kiss this boy, designed to be held by him.

All the careful postures I held melted away, and I pulled him to me, wishing there was a way to be even closer.

We were stars. We were music. We were time.

When we pulled apart, I was overcome with a delicious dizziness. I felt as if I were a different person, like my skin even hung on my bones in a new way. My saltwater blood was sparkling through me, and I was more alive than I'd ever been.

"Wow," I breathed.

Instantly, I was aware of my mistake. Akinli's eyes

drooped, and he shook his head as if he was trying to clear it.

"Akinli!" I cried stupidly, trying to pull him from the daze.

He lost his balance, falling into me, then staggered upright and moved past me, toward the Ocean.

I raced after him, wrapping my arms around him, trying to hold him back. "NO!" I shouted, but he didn't even glance at me, just continued ceaselessly toward Her. He walked steadily into the Ocean, and I followed, trying desperately to pull him back on land. Thank goodness there were no rocks here or they would have ripped him to shreds as he blindly strode into the water.

Her waves lapped around my ankles, then my knees. I yanked with all my strength, hating myself for thinking all this time that I had been stronger than any human. My waist dipped into the cold water, and my shoulders, too. Was the water so cold that it could hurt him? My skin couldn't judge that anymore. I tugged and tugged, because all he had left now was his ability to breathe.

Then, unhesitating, he dived beneath Her waters. Still, I followed.

19

er voice was loud in my ear.

You didn't answer Me! Your sisters have been worried! What in the world have you been doing?

Ignoring Her, I wrapped my arms around Akinli's chest. His eyes were open, blinking, but completely unfocused.

Let him go.

I tugged. *No. I have to get him to air,* I thought back.

He heard your voice. He's Mine.

I couldn't pull Akinli up. There was tension, as if a rope were holding him to the sandy Ocean floor.

I beg You. Spare him.

His death will let others live.

And yet I would bring You thousands in exchange for him, I vowed. *Please. Let him live. Please.*

I could feel Her grip on him, still firm. His eyes had closed, and I was running out of time. *He* was running out of time.

Between my behavior during the last sinking and risking our exposure, I knew I'd already pushed past Her limits. I had never disobeyed Her before, not in eighty-one years. And I was asking for far too much right now. I had no doubt that however this ended, punishment would be waiting for me. I didn't care. For once—just once—I needed to keep someone alive. I begged the Ocean wordlessly, opening my desperate thoughts to Her.

The Ocean fell silent, but suddenly the tension disappeared. I pulled Akinli with all my might. There was no audible gasp when we got to the surface, and I worried that I was already too late. Was he breathing?

She wasn't helping me when I swam, not in the way She usually did, and it was an effort to keep Akinli's head above water as I struggled to get us back to shore. I had thought my body was impenetrable, strong. But I was seriously weakened and exhausted by the time I dragged him up onto the beach.

Harder than I meant to, I dropped his body to the ground, squealing a little when his head bounced off the hard-packed sand. If he wasn't dead, he was very deeply unconscious, because he didn't respond at all.

Please, I thought. *Please, be alive.*

I lowered my ear to his chest and heard the most beautiful sound in the world: Akinli's heartbeat. I moved back and saw he was breathing, though his only motion was the slight rise and fall of his chest.

My heart ached, a physical pain in my chest. He'd lost so much, was still suffering from his parents' death. I hated to abandon him, alone and unconscious in the shadow of the home he'd just offered me. But I needed to go back.

I kissed his wet cheek, hot tears running down my face. "I'm sorry," I cried, touching his face one last time. "This is all I can do for you now. Please live. I love you."

It took every ounce of strength left in my body to rip myself from Akinli's side and fling myself into the surf.

Her waters created a viselike grip around my arm, and She pulled me away before I could think twice. I watched the boats moored in Port Clyde until they were just blackened stars on the horizon.

I was expecting death. Her guiding was so deliberate, I assumed I was being taken to a gallows of sorts. I quietly rejoiced that the others wouldn't see. I didn't want another Ifama burned into Miaka's memory.

She took me so deep that the anticipation of dying became overwhelming. Trying to push away my rising panic, I fixed my thoughts on Akinli, knowing he'd wake up eventually and be fine. I remembered all the little pieces of our day, wanting his kindness to be the last thought in my head as I went to my grave.

This is why I don't take wives. You will never serve Me properly now. And see how you ache? Your little infatuation did this to you. I could feel Her anger all around me.

Can You please kill me quickly? I asked, starting to cry. *I'm afraid.*

I'm not ending your life. Not today.

Finally, She released me onto the pitch-black of the Ocean floor. I knew I was hopelessly trapped. Her currents would never let me rise to the surface. I'd wander in Her depths forever.

You've nearly exposed yourself and your sisters twice!

I recoiled at the anger in Her voice.

You made the bride you so desperately wanted to protect suffer far longer than she needed to. You stopped singing, which alone is enough reason for Me to kill you.

I know, I answered, terrified. *I know.*

Then I riffle through your memories with this boy, your little daydreams, and I see every single risk you've taken in the last day. There were a thousand moments when you encouraged them to wonder about you. You were on the verge of forgetting who you are and speaking so many times. You could have killed them all.

I wept openly, thinking of Ben at the bottom of a bathtub or Julie throwing herself under the kitchen faucet.

What's worse, you took what was rightfully Mine. He ought to have died tonight.

You said you weren't killing me. Is that true? I doubled over in sadness, hardly able to think through it all. *I've broken Your rules. I know the penalty for that. And I will tell You plainly that if I had to pull Akinli from Your hands a hundred times, I'd do it. I understand Your suffering, but I cannot be the balm for it!*

My hands were shaking. My tears mixed with the salt of Her waters and vanished.

I fear I will spend the next nineteen years disappointing You. I don't want to compromise You in my sisters again, and I don't know how to bear the pain of being separated . . .

I covered my mouth, dejected over my new reality. For, as surely as the sun set in the west, She would keep me from Akinli until one of us died.

I know the consequences of what I've done. Kill me if You must.

There was a long silence, and I could sense Her softening, that strange affection She shared with me above the others.

Do you think I rejoice in death?

I raised my head. *What?*

There is no joy for Me in punishing you or in taking lives. I do what I must to survive. And not only would I not delight in your death, I would mourn it. You must know by now how dear you are to Me.

I swallowed. *Why me? Why do I have Your favor more so than the others?*

She was so tender with me, lifting me up from the sand as if She were cradling a baby. Considering her timelessness and my temporariness, I practically was a newborn in Her eyes.

Throughout My many, many years and all the sirens I've carried in My hands, none of them has considered Me as you do. There's been a detachment, a deliberate isolation between them and Me.

But you? You come to Me with a sweetness, an attempt to understand. You come to Me even when you are not called. I feel for you what a mother feels for her daughter. To end your life would be to end Mine.

I cried again. *I'm so sorry. I never wanted to hurt You.*

I know. Which is why you shall stay. But you know as well as I do that you cannot come away from this unscathed. Miaka and Elizabeth walk a fine line, and if they thought they could live however they liked with no repercussions, I fear for what would happen.

I trembled. There was far too much truth to that.

I understand. So what happens now?

She deliberated, searching for a suitable alternative.

Fifty more years.

What?

I'm adding fifty years to your time.

No! I pleaded. *No, You can't do that!*

I cannot bear to kill you. I've just explained how precious you are to Me. Would it be so awful for us to have more time together?

Please, no! Don't make me live nearly seventy years more without him.

Her tone soured. *Heed My warning. Banish him from your thoughts. I don't want to end your life, and I wouldn't want a reason to end his. . . .*

She let the sentence hang, and I found myself paralyzed. His life depended on my obedience.

He spent so much time on the wall

No! You can't! No!

I was jettisoned upward as I heard Her call for my sisters.

Please don't do this!

You will come to terms with this eventually, She assured me. *It's better than you deserve.*

I can't. My spirit was so weak. *I can't.*

We'll speak soon. When you're ready.

Please.

She left me on a thin beach covered with small rocks and debris. Picking up my hands and seeing the sludge on my skin made it seem as though I'd been left in a pile of trash. Was that what I was now? Truthfully, it didn't feel that far off.

20

I looked around, trying to make sense of where I was. Even in the pitch-black of night, the sky had a strange glow. I heard the rumble of cars and realized I was under a bridge.

I turned at the sound of running feet and saw familiar silhouettes. My sisters were rushing toward me. Behind them, New York City was ablaze.

They searched the narrow shore, double-checking that we were alone. Padma knelt beside me first.

"Are you okay?"

I shook my head.

"We were worried about you." Elizabeth fell to her knees in front of me. "You stopped singing, and then you just left. Where have you been?"

I shook my head again, tears running down my face.

"What's wrong?" Miaka asked.

"Are we safe?" I asked between sobs.

"Yes," she assured me. "We're under the Manhattan Bridge. There aren't many people out this late, and the noise of the cars will drown us out, so we're fine."

"Where *were* you?" Elizabeth's hands were on her hips as she got to her feet, frowning. "The Ocean told us that She was searching but you wouldn't answer."

Miaka put her hand on my shoulder comfortingly. "We know the cruise ship upset you. But you didn't have to leave." I winced, nauseous at the memory of the bride's face—Karen's face—and of everything I'd been trying to outrun while I'd been with Akinli. Nothing had changed.

I took in a few deep breaths. "Gag me," I begged.

"What?" Padma asked.

"Gag me. Please!"

Elizabeth ripped off her shirt and wrapped it around my face. I held it tightly against my mouth and let out the loudest scream my tiny body could make. The guttural rawness of it was such a departure from our pretty little voices, and it felt honest, more like who I really was. I didn't know how else to release the pain.

"Kahlen?" Miaka pleaded.

I slowly pulled away the shirt. "She gave me fifty more

years. Fifty years onto my sentence."

Elizabeth cursed and Padma gasped.

Miaka embraced me. "I'm so sorry. But at least you're still alive."

"Am I?"

Miaka started walking. "Come on. Let's get inside."

Under the blanket of night, we settled into a brownstone in Brooklyn. While the others unpacked their clothes and rearranged the new furniture, I wept in an empty corner on the floor. Two full days I spent in tears. And when it felt like all the water was out of my body, I finally fell asleep.

With Padma's enthusiasm driving them, the girls became tourists. They went to the Statue of Liberty and as many Broadway shows as they could get tickets for. They looked for reviews of restaurants and clubs, turning Padma into another party girl. I sighed to myself, not ready to spend who knew how many more years watching this endless cycle of drinking and dancing and hunting. It felt like, despite my punishment, they'd forgotten all about me or how I might take to this kind of living. We were together as we'd always been, but I'd never felt more alienated.

On one of their many evenings out, I found myself digging through my trunk.

I looked at all those scrapbooks. I wasn't going to do it again. Knowing Karen's name was bad enough, but I had no desire to learn the names of her parents or of her flower girl. No amount of information could atone for what I'd done. When had it ever?

I lifted the trunk and carted it outside. We weren't that far from the bridge or the water, though it took some work to get it down to that narrow shore.

I stood there, bare feet gripping the rocks, and hurled each of the scrapbooks into the water.

Good-bye, Annabeth Levens, and your faith in four-leaf clovers.

Good-bye, Marvin Heirholm, and your three-time-winning rec baseball league.

Good-bye to thousands and thousands of lives that I couldn't fix and that couldn't fix me.

I threw my brush, some dresses I'd been hanging on to, and all my papers on sirens into the water. What was the point anymore?

The last thing I came upon was my bobby pin, the one connection I had to my mother. I flipped it over in my fingers, watching my hand as it slowly streaked orange with rust. Then I flicked it into the water.

Nothing was holding on to me anymore, and there was nothing left to hold on to.

In the following weeks, the girls didn't notice that my trunk was gone, which said something, considering how tight our quarters were. For me, it was further proof that I was becoming invisible to them, little more than a rock that dragged them down.

New York was a new kind of magic for Elizabeth and Miaka. A city that never sleeps was a perfect fit for girls who never slept either. And while Padma followed them, participating in their endless desire to see every little thing, I could see her wearing down under the weight of their adventures until one night it was too much.

"You can't stay in," Elizabeth insisted. "This place is supposed to be the hottest club in the whole city."

Padma playfully rolled her eyes. "So was the one we went to yesterday."

Elizabeth shrugged. "It only takes a day for it to change. Come on, you can't miss this!"

"Leave her be," Miaka urged. "Padma hasn't been a siren that long, and I feel sure her life before this wasn't anywhere near this fast paced."

Padma unfolded a hand toward Miaka. "Thank you. No, it wasn't. So a night off will do me good. Besides, Kahlen could use the company."

I'd been hearing their conversation but only really tuned in when I heard my name. Peeking over from my corner on the couch, I saw all their eyes on me. How nice of them to remember I was still here.

"Huh?"

"You wouldn't mind if I stayed in with you tonight, would you?" Padma's eyes were pleading.

I mustered up a smile, feeling bad for Padma. She was only following the others' example in how she lived, in how she responded to me. Her life as a siren to date had not been the experience I'd wanted to give her. "Not at all."

Elizabeth sighed. "Fine. Suit yourself."

Within twenty minutes they were gone, and Padma had settled on the opposite end of the couch in leggings and an oversize shirt. She had disengaged from her old style of dress so quickly it made me feel broken again, so slow to change.

"Thanks," she mumbled. "It's fun to go out and see new things, but it's a lot to take in."

"I understand. I tried to get into their lifestyle, going out for drinks and dancing. I did it once," I said, holding up a finger. "I gave up right after."

Padma laughed. "I can't imagine you in one of those dresses, shaking your hips on a dance floor."

I grinned. "Exactly. It wasn't for me. I'm more . . ." I almost said I was more of a jitterbug kind of girl, but the thought took me four hundred miles north. " . . . more of a homebody."

"I like it. There's something electric about being awake in the night and all those strangers around you. It can be very distracting." Her expression shifted. "I wish it lasted longer."

I focused, seeing the past few weeks afresh. I'd been so worried about my suffering that I completely forgot about hers.

"You still remember it all, don't you?"

She nodded. "I went to the Ocean a few days ago, and I tried to let Her carry away my thoughts."

"I'm not sure that's how it works."

"Yeah," she said, fidgeting with the hem of her shirt. "I guess not." She stared at the floor unhappily.

I was failing her. She suffered in her own way and still had a century in front of her. How was her pain any less valid than mine? The source was different, but I'd ignored it in favor of my own.

I scooted a little closer. "Listen, I'm sorry. I know I've been kind of checked out lately."

"It's okay," she said. "I cried for hours once the sinking was over. Miaka said I'd grow stronger, but I don't know. Either way, I understand how hard it was for you to take those lives. And then the Ocean giving you more time when you're so close to the end . . . You deserve the chance to deal with what you're feeling."

My eyes brimmed with tears. "Thank you for understanding. All the same, I'm sorry I haven't been a better sister to you."

"It sounds like you've been keeping things together for decades. I don't blame you. I just wish I knew how to do this as well as everyone else. Kahlen, you're the oldest. Can't you tell me how to forget?" she implored. Suddenly, she burst out crying. "I can't carry this weight anymore. Please. It hurts too much."

I embraced her, holding her tight. "I don't know what to tell you. It will fade, I promise. But even if, for some horrible reason, you end up holding on to these memories for the next hundred years, the day you are no longer a siren, it will all be over forever."

"Yeah?"

"Of course. Do you think you'd be able to live your life knowing the Ocean ate humans? That you'd spent a century helping Her do that? Everything goes. It's like you get three lives. One with no idea how to live it, one with more power than anyone could imagine, and one with a true sense of self and the ability to pursue anything you want."

She wiped at her tears. "That's a small comfort. But it's so far away."

I smiled sadly. "I know, but don't worry. Soon your memories will go. I swear. There's no reason they should stay."

We were quiet for a while as she took that in, but I could see it was still haunting her.

"I hate him, Kahlen," she whispered. "He treated me

like trash, and he tried to kill me. And my mother sat by, letting it happen. So I hate her, too."

"You have to let it go. Hate makes it stay."

"What if there's no room for love?" she asked quietly, laying her head on my shoulder.

"Don't be silly." I wrapped my arm around her. "There's always room for love. Even if it's as small as a crack in a door. That will be enough."

Two weeks later, a homeless man attacked Elizabeth. She whispered in his ear to get him off her, and he threw himself into the Hudson. Not wanting to stick around, everyone packed up their possessions once again.

Not me. From now on, I carried nothing.

21

An abandoned estate on an island off of Italy.
A small house near a fishery in Mexico.
A rental unit on the Olympic Peninsula.
Different names for the same place.

Four locations over the course of seven months was a lot for us, more than a lot. Though Elizabeth was the catalyst for the initial move, I could tell they'd all decided I needed space, needed a place where I could speak out loud without worrying about being overheard. I thought it must have been Padma's doing, encouraging the moves to peaceful scenery and isolated locations. My sisters were hoping a change of setting would snap me out of my depression. And while I appreciated it, nothing they did could help me.

As soon as I could manage it, I'd go live alone somewhere. It didn't matter where. I was tired of trying to be something I wasn't, and I was tired of feeling like a burden to my sisters on top of everything I felt for myself.

Our current home was a large lake house, with a grassy slope that eventually turned into rounded rocks and led into the Ocean. It was isolated and had only a single, well-worn dirt road leading up to it. If we needed to get to anything or anyone, it would take a solid half hour.

My sisters chose well. The ability to speak in open air was good for me, though it couldn't cure my longing for Akinli or my sorrow over my punishment. The Ocean tried to talk to me, but I ignored Her call, grimly satisfied that She couldn't hear me if I stayed on land. Instead, I spent hours watching massive birds swoop down and pluck their meals from the water and listening to the sound the wind made as it punched its way through the trees.

It brought me no joy. In fact, until now, I hadn't had a single reason to laugh since the moment I'd left Akinli's side. What made me giggle on this otherwise inconsequential day was the extraordinary sensation on my leg.

It was itchy.

I was hypnotized by the feeling, the irritating warmth on my calf. I stared at the spot, just barely pink, which was also strange—our skin was usually as unchanging and impervious to harm as the rest of us—but I was thankful for it.

Of all the exotic foods and beautiful places shared, of all the diversions and stories offered, this tiny little novelty made me feel like there was a part of me somewhere that was still human.

"Kahlen?"

I looked over my shoulder to see Miaka bringing me a mug of tea. I stayed on my rock, thinking of how we were separated from the Ocean and yet surrounded by Her. I'd seen Her so many different ways: flat as paper, impatient as a child, alive as a party. Right now, all She could be to me was an enemy.

"Penny for your thoughts?" Miaka asked, settling in beside me.

"If I could arrange them into a proper line, I'd tell you."

Miaka smiled, sipping from her own mug. "How do you like it here?"

"It's fine."

"Fine? Kahlen, we're doing our best to help."

I stared into the endless day. I kept waiting, like Padma, for time to ease my ache. So far, that wasn't happening.

"I don't know what to tell you. Maybe you guys should go back to a city and leave me. I'm just going through something, I guess."

Miaka nodded her head toward the water. "She's

worried about you. Surely you can tell."

I nodded. "She thinks I'm being petulant, that I'll get over it. I can feel that." I held the mug in my hand, taking in its warmth. "Truth is, I don't know how to forgive Her."

"It's better than death."

"It doesn't feel that way."

"You are brave, Kahlen, and very smart. You can make it through seventy years."

"It's not just that. . . ." I sat up, exhausted from holding it in, and looked her square in the eyes. "I met a boy."

Miaka gazed at me in confusion. "In one day?"

"No." I wiped at my face, forcing away tears before they could fall. "I met him just over a year ago. He was going to school at the college we were living by in Miami. I met him in the library. Even though I couldn't speak, he'd talk to me, make me feel like an actual person.

"The day I stopped singing, I went to his hometown. His parents had died, and he had to drop out of school."

"Oh, no." She put her hand to her heart. "Does he have any family?"

"He's living with a cousin and his wife. They actually let me into their house for a night, even acted like I could stay indefinitely if I needed to. They took me in like a stray cat."

"If they were that nice, why'd you leave so soon?"

I hid my eyes, ashamed.

"Akinli and I spent the day together. By the end of it, I was lost. Head over heels. He asked me to stay with him, and I thought I could do it. If I was smart, I could be by his side for years. It wouldn't be everything, but we could at least be together.

"A second later, he kissed me. And I spoke. He was song drunk and walked straight into the water."

"Kahlen!"

"I know. He was supposed to die, but I begged the Ocean to let him live. I got him back onto shore, and She punished me with life instead of death. And now his life depends on my behavior. He's a fisherman and on the water all the time. She's made it very clear that if I step out of line because of him, She'll eliminate him from the equation."

Miaka shook her head in disbelief. "Why would She do that to you? She *loves* you."

"It sounds crazy, but She seemed jealous," I confessed. "Like he couldn't have my affection because it was Hers."

"But threatening you won't bring Her your love."

"She's not human," I reminded her. "I'm not sure She understands all our relationships."

It might have been the closest I'd ever seen Miaka get to being angry. She scrunched her face together, frustrated at my situation in spite of my stupidity in letting it happen in the first place.

"I won't tell the others," she said after a moment. "I think it would rile Elizabeth, and Padma's so young she follows Elizabeth's lead in everything."

"She'll figure out who she is soon enough."

Miaka sighed. "I hope so. For now, I don't think this information needs to be shared."

I nodded, my mind on the other side of the country. "He was sweet, you know? It felt like a really special thing, to find someone so kind."

Miaka pushed her forehead playfully against mine. "I can't imagine you risking everything for anyone who wasn't worthy."

I drew her to me and hugged her quickly, grateful she understood. But as much as I appreciated my sister's support, I wished Aisling were there. She had known what it was to love someone who you knew would grow old without you.

When there's no need to sleep, no need to eat, when there's nothing but empty years lying in wait, the soul becomes restless. I had been thinking about Aisling's choices, and I understood why she had watched her family from afar. But she and I were different creatures, with different relationships with the people we left behind.

I had spent days considering how Aisling had lived. In the end, I knew one absolute truth: I could never go back to Akinli.

My last wish for him was that he'd have a long and happy life, and I meant that with all that was within me. But watching him forget me, seeing him with some other girl, seeing his face in their children . . . I couldn't stomach it.

I also knew I couldn't forget him. But that was a cross I would have to bear in silence.

Silence. I ought to be used to that by now.

22

Miaka's brushes were scattered on the floor. She'd been painting nonstop for days.

"That's a pretty one," I commented, hoping that line would be enough conversation to get me through the rest of the day without my sisters looking at me with big, worried eyes when they thought I couldn't see them.

"Thanks. The last few have been a bit rougher, yeah?"

I nodded.

"I like your aggressive ones," Elizabeth said. "I think people would laugh if they knew something so menacing came out of a sixteen-year-old."

"Or an eighty-seven-year-old. Either way."

They giggled, but I saw nothing comical about it.

"Can I make art, too?" Padma asked. It was sweet. I could still see the tension in her eyes, feel that she wasn't free of her worries, but she was trying to tackle them any way she could. She was stronger than I was, and I admired her for it.

"Me, too!" Elizabeth said, grabbing at a stack of papers.

"Sure." Miaka rolled her hair up into a bun, spearing it with a colored pencil. "Be grand, be fearless. Make something people can't look away from."

"I don't think I can re-create myself." Elizabeth wiggled her eyebrows.

"But who could?"

I gave them a smile, a dim, tiny thing. I remembered thinking in Port Clyde that I could live my life for Akinli. I wondered now if I could go back to trying to live for my sisters. After all, they were all I had left in the world. But I simply couldn't drum up the will.

As I focused on the lines of the floorboards, Miaka wordlessly set some paper and charcoal pencils in front of me. She met my gaze and shrugged.

"I hurt, too. Not the same as you, I know that. But this helps me. Maybe . . . maybe . . ."

I placed a hand on hers. "Thank you."

She walked back to her canvas, determined to finish a collection. I wasn't worried about having a home anymore, or new clothes, but Elizabeth and Miaka very much were. I knew they felt responsible for Padma and, now, for me, too. For the time being, I was going along with whatever they wanted, simultaneously wanting to be alone while hoping they wouldn't kick me out of their circle for being too miserable.

If I were left to my own devices, I might try to go back to Maine. I wasn't strong enough to keep a safe distance on my own yet. And I was afraid. If I made a mistake, it would ruin Akinli. And there was a corner of my heart that worried the Ocean might rid me of him for the sake of security, or for whatever reason seemed most believable to Her.

I pulled over the paper and doodled. It was nothing. Pages of circles and zigzags. But on one page the curve of a line turned into the profile of Akinli's cheek, and the circles were the exact shapes of his eyes.

I was no artist, but I'd committed every piece of Akinli to memory, and he spilled out onto the page whether I liked it or not. It was remarkable, really, what my hands were capable of. They could remember the way it felt to touch his hair, the prickle of end-of-the-day stubble, the warm curve of his chin, and they re-created it beautifully in black and white.

How I missed that face. What wouldn't I give to see it light up in surprise or conspire with me through a wink?

That face had so quickly become the symbol of comfort in my world.

I didn't want to cry in front of the others, not with their worry constantly hovering over me as it was. Instead, I balled up the papers and tossed them into the trash.

I tried to do the same with my memories, but it did no good. How would I ever be able to get past this?

I walked out the back door, down the slope, and to the one place I'd been avoiding for months.

Welcome. The Ocean sounded tentative, but as if She was happy to see me. Her waters embraced me as I waded deeper, then lay back, floating.

This isn't working, I confessed, sinking.

What?

Separating me from someone I love doesn't make me love You more. It makes me bitter. I don't want to exist like this, like half a person.

You aren't, She insisted. *You're more than a person. I've bestowed on you everything I can. You are stronger than anyone. You have My favor above anyone before you. What more do you want?*

To fall in love, I admitted. *To get married.*

Which you will certainly be able to do once you no longer belong to Me.

But Akinli will be dead! Or very close to! Whatever You may think of humans, it isn't acceptable to wed a corpse!

Why would you think I have a low opinion of humans? She asked, irritation in Her voice. *I live to serve them. Everything I am is theirs. You think you have some heavy curse on you, what of Me?*

She waited for an answer that I didn't have.

Is it too much to ask that I keep the one precious thing I've had a little while longer?

I was silent. I thought of my life, both the few years I was truly flesh and blood and the decades of being something much more frightening. There was nothing special about me, nothing changed by me living or dying. For Her, not surviving wasn't an option.

I thought of my sadness, brought on by my own foolishness and prolonged by my stubbornness. She didn't have the option of being low, of not constantly giving.

When I measured up everything, I was insignificant. Except maybe to Her.

You think more time is a punishment, but you can continue to grow, to learn. Why do you want to leave Me?

That's not at all what I'm saying. Why didn't She get this?

What are you saying?

I gritted my teeth, frustrated and furious. *Do You understand how difficult it is for me to love You when You threaten someone I care about? You know how flawed I am. How can I trust that You won't destroy him the next time I fall short?*

You've served so well, Kahlen. You never made a misstep until you met him. The more you speak of this boy, the surer I feel his death would benefit you.

No! I could feel anger and fear radiating from my skin. *Don't You understand? This makes me hate You!*

Then where is our balance? How do we commune together now, after such a mistake?

I closed my eyes, wounded by the word. Akinli was no mistake.

Control your thoughts.

You want my devotion? My undying affection?

Yes. As you have Mine.

Then don't threaten me with his death, I said. *Promise me his life.*

How do you mean?

I thought over what I knew about Her. *You can identify certain souls if You must, yes?*

Of course.

Then promise me that if You see his struggling body in water, You will bring it to shore. Promise me that if a rope pulls him off his boat, You'll untangle it Yourself. Promise me that my voice will never bring him to his grave. If You do all that, if You can spare him, then I'll never say his name again. Swear his safety to me, and I will give You all that's left of me.

She considered this. *Will you be kinder to your sisters? They worry.*

I give You my word. Miaka, Elizabeth, and Padma will have the best of my spirits.

I could feel Her waves moving like gears, processing the request and searching for a flaw.

I promise.

Then I promise, too, She vowed. *Akinli's death will not come at My hands. Furthermore, I'll do everything I can to prevent it.*

The tension in my body slackened, a fear finally removed.

Thank You.

I will be here when you are ready to love Me. Go to your sisters. They need you as well.

I left the water, marching back to the house dripping wet. Miaka and Elizabeth were leaning together at the table, conspiring as usual while Padma watched them, her chin cupped in her hands.

"Hey!" Miaka said brightly. "We were thinking of trying to find a new city, someplace warm. Any suggestions?"

"We don't have to leave. I told you, it's fine here. At this rate, we'll run out of places to go."

"All the same," Elizabeth said. "Where did you go when you left us for that day? Anywhere good?"

It felt as if a nail went through my heart. It hadn't been good. It had been perfect. "Port Clyde. It's this tiny town in Maine. We'd never blend in there."

"Oh." Elizabeth pursed her lips, thinking.

I watched the puddle at my feet blossom. "I know what you're doing."

Miaka froze. "What do you mean?"

"Hopping from place to place, trying to fix me. I appreciate it, but it's not going to make things better."

Elizabeth stood. "We just don't know what else to do. You've taken care of us for so long, and we want to do the same for you."

These were big words, considering her fixation on her own comfort and happiness. I sighed, remembering what I'd just promised the Ocean, and walked over to my sisters embracing them. "It's a season," I told them. "Every season ends."

I pushed a smile onto my face. I'd made a vow, and I always obeyed. That had been my talent in this life, and I needed to readopt it.

"That season ends today. I simply needed time to adjust. I'll be fine now."

The lie took so much energy out of me. That would be fine. My body, at least, was indestructible.

23

"Hey, prom queen," he began, laughing.

I grinned in spite of myself. "That's not even a funny joke anymore."

"Well, you're stuck with it now."

I rolled into him on the blanket we were sharing. We rested on the patch of grass between his house and the water. The sun was blinding, and I was calmed by the hush of water hitting the sand.

Akinli smelled of cotton and grass and something dry . . . maybe books. It was a wonderfully unique scent, and I was intoxicated by it.

"So what do you want to study?" He held up a pamphlet in front of me. "English? Communication? Remember when we met and you were looking at all those cakes?"

"Mmm, cake," I answered dreamily.

Akinli chuckled in reply. "You could study culinary arts. What do you think about that?"

"I'd eat every assignment. I'd have nothing left for the professor to grade."

He swatted me with the paper. "Well, what then? When I go back, you're going with me. What do you want to study?"

"Maybe history," I confessed.

"You sound ashamed."

"It just doesn't sound as exciting as being a chemist or a lawyer. I'd probably end up in a museum or something."

Akinli shrugged. "Who cares? If you're happy, then that's all that matters."

I can show you history!

We both sat upright.

"Whoa!"

"Did you hear that?" I asked. He shouldn't have heard anything. Nor should I, not anymore.

I can take you across centuries. Stay with Me.

"But I already did!" I cried. I hadn't forgotten. Everything I'd been promised was false.

"Who is that? Who are you talking to?"

Stay. I can give you everything.

She'd gotten stronger, much stronger, and I imagined

Her forcing tsunamis and pulling down airplanes just to have the energy for this moment. The wind pushed me toward the Ocean and kept Akinli rooted in place.

Look! He's safe. Just as I promised. Now come home.

"No! No, I gave you all my time!"

"Kahlen!" Akinli reached for me, his face agonized.

I jerked awake. Sleep had seemed like a good idea, a way to pass hours without disappointing or lying to my sisters. Weirdly enough, there were even days lately when I had felt as if I *needed* rest. For now, it would have to be avoided. I couldn't shake the dream of Akinli hearing the Ocean, understanding Her call. It gave me a chill.

When my heart rate dropped, I went hunting for the girls. It was daybreak, and the sun shone harshly through the windows. Elizabeth's honey-brown hair was extra golden in the morning light.

"Hi," I said, coming up to her. She had a wide canvas on the floor and had switched from paintbrushes to brooms. Padma sat quietly, watching her. My youngest sister had said less and less as the days passed, but she seemed content with Elizabeth. I watched as Elizabeth swept the broom across the canvas, leaving a wide streak of blue. "That's one way to do it, I guess."

She laughed. "I'm not as gifted as Miaka. I can't do all that fine-tip stuff. But this? This feels like me."

I took in the garish strokes, the haphazard color choices.

Everything looked as if it could almost be an accident, but you could feel the heart behind it. "It absolutely does. Where's Miaka?"

"Oh, she's out," Elizabeth hedged, something slightly off in her voice.

"Out where?"

"She read about some forest in Iceland that has these really special flowers. If you grind the petals and mix them with oil, it's supposed to make this crazy, vibrant paint. Like, better than anything you could buy in a store."

"Oh. So, how long will that take her?"

"A few days, I guess. The Ocean took her to Iceland, but she has to find the actual flowers herself."

I stared at the finished paintings scattered around our living room. Miaka had over a dozen now, enough to call a collection and start selling.

"I wish she'd have taken us with her. I could use a project right now."

"Then paint something," Elizabeth suggested, dipping her broom into a vat of yellow.

"Not sure I have anything worth making right now."

"Don't be silly. Find the right billionaire, and he'll buy a streak of green paint on an otherwise blank page for enough to cover three months' rent."

She grinned as she went back to her work.

I sat down with the charcoals again and tried, I really

did. But everything that came out was either the waves of Akinli's hair when he drove with the window down or his still hands when I pulled his body out of the water. I stayed away from his face, but he came back to me in a hundred different images. They were nothing but rough scratches across the paper, but I left them in a pile for Miaka. She could decide what to do with them.

When she finally returned four days later, fresh out of the water, I was pleased with how much potential she saw in my sloppy little scribbles.

"There's something very honest about them, Kahlen. If I had the money, I'd buy them off you right now."

I hit her arm. "Stop it. I like them, but they're not that good. Nothing like what you make."

"Well, I'm still going to put them in my showcase."

"Along with the new stuff? With your flower paint?"

She squinted. "Huh?"

"The flowers from Iceland. Aren't you making paint?"

She laughed and waved a carefree hand at me. "Oh, I couldn't even find them. I felt like such a dope wandering around in the woods for all that time. I think a little more research is in order."

"I'll come with you next time if you want."

Miaka touched my arm. "That's really sweet of you. It's nice to see a little bit of Kahlen coming back."

I shrugged. "Don't give up on me. I'm trying."

"Never." Miaka winked at me as I walked to the kitchen. Maybe a little food would boost our collective spirits. Maybe it would fill the hole in my stomach that felt like an eerie hunger.

As I turned to open the refrigerator, I noticed Miaka give Elizabeth a minuscule nod. Elizabeth inhaled deeply, trying to hide a smile.

Elizabeth went out back to hose off her brooms, and Miaka left to find dry clothes, and nothing more came of the exchange.

A few weeks later, Elizabeth went on a five-day shopping trip. Padma cried, begging her not to leave, but to no avail. Elizabeth insisted it was necessary. Elizabeth had done this a few times in the past, buying so many clothes, she shipped them home instead of carrying them. This time she returned with two bags. Two!

"What can I say? Everything's dreadful this season," she said, tossing her finds in a corner as if they didn't even matter.

After that, Miaka spent a week in Japan reconnecting with her roots for the sake of her art. The entire time she was gone, Elizabeth did nothing but pace from room to room, never settling, as if she couldn't stand her absence. Personally, I didn't understand the trip in the first place. Miaka had never wanted to go home before, no matter the reason. And when she came back, it looked like the same old art to me.

I didn't even try to remember Elizabeth's next excuse for leaving, though I didn't understand her reasons either. If she'd been so antsy for Miaka to get back and knew how upset Padma got when she left, why did she go?

When she returned, I pounced on them all, determined to end this.

"Why do you keep running off?" I demanded, planting my hands on my hips.

Miaka crossed her arms defensively. "I don't know what you mean."

"I feel like I'm doing a lot better, like I'm much easier to be around. So why do you keep taking turns bailing and leaving Padma to babysit me?"

"No one is babysitting you," Elizabeth argued, throwing herself down on the couch. "We've just been thinking it would be nice to spend time alone occasionally. Like Aisling used to."

Padma jumped on board. "Yeah."

My eyes bounced between them, having a difficult time imagining that was true. Elizabeth and Miaka had been inseparable for decades, and it seemed like Padma fit right in. Why now? What had happened?

"Are you fighting?" I asked, still skeptical.

"No." Elizabeth was dripping all over the couch.

"Are you upset with me?"

Miaka walked over, her expression tender. "No. Not in the slightest. We've been curious about Aisling's method, that's all. But it's strange to stay away for long." She turned to Elizabeth. "I don't know how she went for months."

"Me neither. I'd be miserable without you." Padma nodded. I didn't want to comment that she didn't seem that happy in the first place. One argument at a time.

"So . . . so everything's fine?" I asked. I placed a hand on my forehead, feeling a little dizzy. The same feeling had washed over me three times in the last week, forcing me into bed until my head cleared up.

"Yes."

"Oh." I backed away, my brain muddled from the woozy feeling and the confusion over their absences. "Sorry. Things have been off for me lately."

Miaka smiled. "We know. And we're here for you."

"Or there for you," Elizabeth added, pointing a graceful arm toward the Ocean.

A chill ran through me. When it lingered, I wrapped myself in blankets and retreated to my room, disappointed in myself. Was I becoming paranoid?

I breathed, reminding myself of my promise. I was going to be an exemplary sister. It wouldn't do for me to go around accusing them of things. I needed to take up a hobby or something. There was too much free time, too much space for my mind to wander.

If I was going to keep my promise and try to live without Akinli, I needed to find something else to think about.

A few days later, I was forced to think about someone other than Akinli. We all had to focus on Padma whether we wanted to or not.

"She still can't forget. She wants her father to suffer as she did." Miaka's face was solemn as she faced me across the table. Beside her, tears ran down Padma's face. Elizabeth sat on her other side, her hand lightly on our youngest sister's shoulder.

I felt awful. I'd known she was sad, but I didn't think it was this bad. It had been over a year. We'd already had a second—and more somber—Christmas together and sat watching the ball drop in New York on New Year's Eve. Padma sorrowfully wished she could have been there for that. We were seeing commercials for Valentine's Day now, and Padma was no longer a fresh siren. None of it made sense.

"Why?" I asked. "We all forget our past lives. How can you still remember so much?"

"It's because she's still angry," Elizabeth guessed. My thoughts went back to our brownstone, when a very similar theory had occurred to me. "Miaka's forgiven her family, so she doesn't remember details, and I know you've forgotten almost everything. But I remember more than either of you, and Padma went through so much more than any of us. . . ."

"I remember enough. My parents didn't really appreciate me either," Miaka admitted, looking at Padma. "It wasn't quite as dire as your situation, but it was close."

Padma nodded.

"They might not have rejoiced in my death, but I doubt they mourned," Miaka continued. "If you think that thought hasn't haunted me, you're wrong. We all suffer our regrets." She gestured to each of us.

I nodded. I felt immeasurable guilt over the loss of my family, as if maybe I could have undone it somehow. Then there were the tens of thousands of lives I sang into the grave. I carried them like a weight around my neck.

And, always, probably forever, Akinli.

"But you cannot go seeking revenge," Miaka told Padma firmly.

Padma sighed, wiping away her tears. "It just feels like an injustice. He killed me. My mother let him. No one will come looking for me; no police will come for them. It's not fair!"

Elizabeth shook her head.

"What?" I shot. "You think she should go, don't you?"

Elizabeth shrugged. "If she hadn't told us, if she had gone on her own, it would be done by now, and none of us would have been the wiser."

"The Ocean would have been," I replied. "If Padma had hopped into the water and gone back to India, She certainly would have read her thoughts. The Ocean might have killed her for trying to take revenge." I placed my hand on Padma's arm. "And after what you've been through, to die now? It'd be the greatest loss."

"She could've made it," Elizabeth muttered.

I closed my eyes, trying to keep a hold on my temper.

"I'm sorry for your suffering, Padma," I told her. "You have no idea how much I ache for you. Maybe it's selfish, but I don't need another reason to hate this life. If we lost you now . . ."

I didn't want to think about it.

"What do you mean 'another reason'?" Padma asked. "What else has happened?"

Miaka glanced quickly at me. She had kept what had happened to me—my love, and the bargain I had made with the Ocean—private, waiting for me to be ready to tell the others.

I swallowed. "It's a difficult life," I said dismissively. "You hurt people. You lose people you love."

Elizabeth leaned in. "Who have you loved?"

"I love A . . ." I nearly caved. I missed him so badly. I wondered what he was doing every day. Did he think of me? Was he with someone else? Did he go back to school?

Was he happy? "I loved Aisling. And Marilyn. Eventually, we all get separated. And I loved my family." I smiled to myself. "I was a lucky girl. I was treasured."

Elizabeth seemed disappointed, maybe hoping I'd have something juicy to share, but Miaka spoke up. "You've never talked about them much. I know you had brothers, but that's about it."

I pulled together the few scraps of memory I still had of my family. "I looked like my mother. I can remember a little bit of her face because I see it in mine. And my father was proud of me, mostly because I was beautiful, I think. But he told me often how sharp I was and how easy I was to converse with. And I was obedient." I nodded to myself. "They appreciated that."

"A trait you never lost," Elizabeth commented.

I smirked. "Well, almost never. I've made my share of mistakes, as you've so astutely pointed out."

"And why not?" Elizabeth planted her cheek on her hand, staring me down. "What has this obedience ever gotten you?"

"It has gotten me a second chance, Elizabeth."

She shook her head. "If I had to guess, I'd say it cost you your only chance."

Her words brought back a vaguely familiar feeling . . . the way my body had felt when I fell into the Ocean during my sinking. Hard, sharp, and all too real.

Miaka hit her arm. "Stop it. In case you've forgotten, she's carrying fifty more years on her back right now. You know what she's going through."

Elizabeth rolled her eyes as if it were all nothing. "Sorry."

"What if I asked the Ocean?" Padma proposed. "What if She let me go?"

Elizabeth clapped her hands and pointed. "There's one hell of an idea. Ask the Ocean. I bet if we brought their bodies to Her, She'd be grateful."

Miaka was quiet, considering. "That's possible."

"Kahlen?" Padma asked. "Can we go?"

Who was I to say no?

"You can ask, but we all have to agree that what the Ocean says is final. Whatever it is, we will abide by it and drop it."

"You're assuming She'll say no," Elizabeth accused.

"Yes, I am. I don't know why She'd say yes."

"Then you must agree that if She does, you're coming. We won't leave this all on Padma."

I pulled back, shocked. "That's insane. I refuse to take any life I don't absolutely have to."

Elizabeth glared at me. "I always thought we were all in this. You were the one who preached solidarity and support. And now you're leaving the most damaged of us to fend for herself?"

"I'm not leaving her to anything. The Ocean will never agree."

Elizabeth pushed back her chair. "Let's just see about that."

She led the charge down the snow-covered ground to the water, so sure of herself. She was at our newest sister's side as Padma pleaded her case, vowed the care she would take, and promised to bring the bodies of her parents back to the Ocean in return if she was allowed to avenge her death.

But please! Padma begged. *Can't You see how unfair this is?*

I do. But the secrecy of our world is far more valuable than your revenge. A single misstep could ruin everything. You cannot go.

Padma began crying and rushed out of the water. Elizabeth followed, shaking her head.

Don't let her do anything foolish.

I won't, I promised, knowing that command was for me.

Miaka held my hand as we made our way back to the house. Thank goodness our waterfront home was isolated, because Padma's wails were piercing.

"I'm torn," Miaka said, her own eyes filling with tears. "There were so many times I wished I could show my parents that I wasn't worthless. That I was smart and creative. I wanted them to know what I was capable of. To watch her suffer is so painful."

"The Ocean said Padma had a gentle mind and that she'd already let go of a lot. Eventually, it'll all be gone."

Miaka shook her head. "That makes it a thousand times worse. If she's already let go of so many memories, how much must there have been for her to still feel so victimized?"

Days went by, and Padma's tears carried on. I tried to focus on other things and failed. Miaka's brush hung over the canvas, creating nothing. Elizabeth was undistracted.

It wasn't Padma's crying or Elizabeth's anger that finally wore me down. It was Miaka, who, as always, had found the simple truth in everything. She was right; Padma's past must have been horrific for her to carry on this way. She deserved her revenge.

So I was the one who researched trips to India and chose a direct flight out of Miami. We could have flown from the airport nearest our home in Washington State and not had to drive cross-country, but I felt that the farther we traveled over land from where the Ocean thought we were, the more likely we'd be able to escape Her notice. I was the one who rented the car. And I was the one who begged Padma to quiet herself so we could get to Florida without the Ocean knowing.

24

It had been a year and a half since the last time we'd been in Florida, and I actually felt happy as we crossed the border. Not because I knew what was coming; that was something I dreaded. But because this was where I had met Akinli. It was as if I was completing a circle, coming right back to the start. Maybe just being here would fix something in the very core of me that I worried was irreparable.

"This is us," I said, pulling up to the rental house. "Nothing fancy, but we won't be here for long."

"No, it's great," Elizabeth said, taking in the small house and humid air, a blessed change from the frost. We were inland from the coast, not wanting to get too close to the beach. For our plan to work, we had to be sure there was no chance of any of us dipping even one toe in the Ocean. We had only a month or so left before She'd need to feed again. There had been few shipwrecks this year, and unless a big one came soon, we were going to have to sing a little earlier than usual. She was getting hungrier, and I didn't want to strain Her temper.

We'd pulled in with only hours to spare. The flight was leaving in the morning. We toted in our luggage and gathered in the living room, where I gave them final instructions.

"Here are your tickets." I handed over the papers, each assigned to a fake name and ID. "Padma, this was the best I could do."

She stared at the face on the passport. "This girl's nose is hideous!"

"Which is why you can write down that you had a nose job if anyone asks." I ran my fingers through my hair, feeling frazzled, unsure if I should be hating myself right now or not. "Okay, all you need to do is keep a low profile. Padma, remember it is crucial that you do not speak to anyone at any time." I focused my eyes on hers. "You're so new to this, and it's hard in the beginning to stay silent, but if you really want this, you must."

"I understand." She tucked her passport into the dossier with her tickets.

"I've arranged for transportation once you arrive. Padma, I'm counting on you to be their guide. I marked hotels you can stay at if you need to." I handed Miaka the printed-out map. "It might be best to travel by night, but that's up to you."

"Wait, you're not coming?" Padma asked.

"I can't." I bit at my lips and rubbed my hands together, anxious. "But I'm making this possible for you. Can that be enough?"

Elizabeth put a hand on my knee. "It's more than enough."

I sighed. "Listen. I can't stress the importance of this too much. Whatever you do, use water pulled from a well or a pump. It has to be unconnected to Her, or we're all done. And bury the bodies. Keep them from the water. If She catches us . . ."

Miaka took my hand. "We're smart. We'll watch out for Padma, and we'll keep safe."

I swallowed. My throat was dry, a strange sensation. "I'll wait here for you. Please be careful."

They reorganized their bags for the trip, and I unpacked quietly, doing what I could to make myself comfortable in purgatory.

My natural instinct was to go to the library. He hadn't said anything about returning to school, but after all the time that had passed, I could imagine Akinli back in his khaki pants, pushing his carts of books down the hallway, maybe with his hair cut short again or still wearing it pulled up. I'd been so good for so long that if there was a chance of seeing him just once more, even if I had to hide in the shadows, I had to take it.

But all it took was stepping out the front door for me to know: Akinli wasn't here.

I wasn't sure how I could tell, but I felt certain he was still in Maine. It was a bizarre sensation, like someone had attached us at the wrists with a string. If I focused on that feeling hard enough, I could strangely feel his presence. Or rather, the lack thereof.

Alone in the house, with nothing else to hold my attention, I thought of Aisling, wondering if my older sister was still the master of wisdom in her new school. She was the only reason I had thought it was possible to send the girls across the Ocean undetected. She had proved the Ocean didn't know everything. . . .

I packed my few things, filled the rental car, and drove up the coast.

If I had anyone to explain this to, I'd swear up and down that this wasn't why I came back to the East Coast with the girls, or why I sent them to another country. Truly, it wasn't. I had no interest in gambling with Akinli's life. But

I needed to see his face, shorn or unshaven, sloppy or kempt, hopefully covered in a smile. That was my only goal.

I drove nonstop, even when the weather turned icy, making the trip in just over twenty-five hours. Leaving the car well up the lone road into Port Clyde to begin the rest of the trek on foot, I realized there was one huge flaw in my plan.

My skinny jeans and tank top were not going to protect me from the elements, particularly the one I feared the most. I'd come this far, though, so I resorted to theft. I stole a pair of boots that were drying on someone's porch and used a tarp in someone else's backyard to make a coat. It was enough to get me through the snow on the ground, and I looked up at the fat clouds, hoping they'd hold out just a little bit longer.

I hiked through the snow-laden forests straight toward Ben and Julie's house. My heart sped up when I saw the black shutters through the iced-over branches. The truck was in the driveway, next to the little scooter, but no one came in or out, and there was no sign of life through the windows. I watched the house for the better part of an hour before a gust of wind made a letter taped to the door rustle. I wanted to read it immediately. That note might be all I got.

When no one returned to the house by nightfall, I figured the darkness would be enough to hide me, and I scurried across the road.

Tommy—

Left a message on your phone, but just in case you didn't get it, we had to get to the hospital. Emergency. Leave the box in the back of the truck for me, and I'll take care of stuff when we get back. Not sure how long we'll be gone, but I'll call tonight once we have some answers (if we're lucky this time). Anyway, thanks again. Talk soon.

Ben

I felt a pang of fear for Julie. I remembered how she'd fretted over me when I'd washed up on her doorstep. Was she the one who was ill now? If only I could have stayed, I could be holding her hand right now.

I stepped away from the door, feeling idiotic. I shouldn't be here. I was risking too much. Even though I wanted Akinli to be happy, I'd certainly lose any hope of sanity if he'd blissfully moved on without me. And if he saw me here or I made any kind of mistake, his life was on the line. After everything else, what would losing him do to Ben and Julie? I'd been stupid, impulsive.

I walked past the truck, double-checking that Ben's box was indeed in the bed, and continued back to the car via the woods.

I shook my head, counting myself lucky that Akinli

wasn't here. On the drive up to Maine, I'd told myself that this would be a closing point, the way to seal off the end of my feelings for Akinli and any hope for a relationship between us.

But I knew now, it was more than him I missed. In a matter of hours, Ben and Julie had given me the truest sense of home I'd had in a long time, and as long as I lived this life, the concept would be forever tied to the smell of detergent on Julie's clothes and the hum of their radiator, still running in the spring. I didn't love them the way I loved Akinli, but they were special to me, tied to my thoughts of him, and I wished I could have at least seen one of their faces today.

I'd lived through decades, stayed in more countries than the majority of people could ever visit. The happiest and most comfortable place I'd ever been was on that weathered couch with Akinli's arm across my shoulder.

This wouldn't have ended a chapter. It only would have forced me to turn a page.

I drove back to Florida wondering if I'd made a mistake regardless. I ached with disappointment, my breathing painful—strangely painful, as if I'd been in the cold air a little too long. Yes, the Ocean would never know, and neither would the girls. But there was an undeniable pull in my chest—that piece of invisible string—that made each mile harder and harder to travel.

25

I rubbed at my chest, which still ached, as I waited in the car. Their plane had landed almost an hour ago, and I thought it best to head to our rental house in Washington State as soon as they got through customs and collected their luggage. It would be good to get back before the Ocean realized we had traveled.

I wasn't sure I wanted to know if their trip had been a success. Either way, I felt a small triumph. I'd done something, on my own, and no one knew about it. That sense of privacy made me feel like an individual, less of a servant and more of a girl.

Still, I squealed inside the car when I saw Padma, Elizabeth, and Miaka walk out of the airport. I was so happy to have them back.

When Padma saw me, she dropped her bag and bolted across the lot at top speed, purple-black hair trailing after her. We wrapped our arms around each other, doing our best to keep from laughing.

"Thank you," she whispered into my ear. "Thank you for everything."

"Let's get to the car. Come."

I pulled her away, looking back over my shoulder at a very pleased Miaka and Elizabeth. I tossed the keys Elizabeth's way, tired of driving. Actually, a little tired in general. It had been a long few days.

Once we were secure, I asked the only question that mattered. "The Ocean suspects nothing?"

"No," Miaka vowed. "I listened to Her, and She seemed contently unaware. I was anxious about getting home in time, though. Did you hear Her this morning?"

I nodded. "She's hungry."

"We have to sing again?" Padma asked, biting her lip. I knew she was remembering the disaster our last singing had been.

"Don't worry," I promised, twisting around in the front seat to reassure her. "It's not going to be like last time. That will never happen again."

Elizabeth nodded in agreement, and Miaka reached across the backseat to take Padma's hand. "Things are different now," she said. "We'll do what we have to do."

I lay back and closed my eyes, looking forward to return-ing home. I had been dangerously close to seeing Akinli, and being with my sisters would reinforce my resolve to keep away from him.

The crisp memory of his stubble-covered cheek was the last thing I thought of before I fell asleep.

"Wake up, sleeping beauty!" Miaka's voice dragged me from unconsciousness.

I blinked, squinting into the light. "What?"

"We're home!" I looked up to see our sleek, waterfront house as Elizabeth slammed her car door.

"I slept the whole ride?"

Miaka grinned at me. "Impressive for someone who doesn't even need it."

"That was, what, two days?"

She nodded. "Like I said, impressive." There was a tiny wrinkle of worry between her brows, despite her smile. Even for me, it was weird to have slept so long.

Miaka hopped out into the misty gray of the morning. The sun was like a giant pearly mass hiding behind the clouds, still bright enough to mess with my eyes.

I pulled my suitcase from the trunk and hauled it inside. The others returned to their routine instantly, as if we'd merely stopped to have a conversation. Miaka picked up her paints, hunting for yellows and oranges. I couldn't help but wonder what she'd seen while she was gone and how it would inspire her today.

"Okay," Elizabeth said, pulling Padma to the couch. "Let's see if we can find any of these Bollywood movies you were talking about." She aimed the remote at the TV, typing in a search.

I assumed their trip had been successful. Padma wasn't in tears anymore, and the others seemed calm. I smiled at Padma. As always seemed to happen with the young women who lived with us, it felt as if she'd been a sister the entire time. Rubbing at my eyes, I tried to shake off my lingering sleepiness.

I'd dreamed of Akinli, and it had made me happier. This was how I could keep him, and I would revisit all my thoughts of him, both real and imagined, as long as I was allowed.

"Will it be a cruise ship again?" Padma asked nervously, twisting her hands together.

"We don't know," I told her. "I'll tell you what I told you last time: avoid looking at people's faces. You'll hear things whether you want to or not, but look at anything else. The moon, the water, your dress. It helps."

"And right after, we'll come back home and do whatever you like." Elizabeth stroked Padma's hair soothingly.

"We won't leave this time, will we?" Miaka asked.

I shook my head. "I don't think so. This place is so isolated, no one's bothered us. It's probably the easiest place we've ever lived." Whatever had happened in India, Padma was calmer and seemed settled in our waterfront house. Maybe she finally understood her strength, her immortality. There was so much time left for her.

"Agreed."

"So that's it then," I said to the group. "We'll do our job and come back here. Maybe we can cele— Well, not celebrate, but, you know, do something special."

"We've got some wine," Elizabeth reminded us.

"And more movies," Padma added.

I reached out for her hand. "Fine. Movie night it is."

Come. It's approaching.

Padma peeked over my shoulder at the water and swallowed. "Let's go."

I was proud of her bravery and hoped it held out through the night. Padma kept Elizabeth's hand in hers as she took to the Ocean.

"I feel like your best friend has been stolen," I admitted to Miaka.

"Nah. She still loves me. Like I know you do, even when you're distracted."

"Am I distracted?"

She pursed her lips at me knowingly. "Your head is

somewhere else most days. But I don't blame you. And I don't blame Elizabeth for taking Padma under her wing. They'll be together the longest."

I sighed. "Not anymore."

She tugged at my arm. "Come on. It's time."

We dived in, catching the current that would take us to the ship right away. The salt tickled as it stuck to me, making my dress. It was such an old routine, I could nearly do it without thinking. Until somewhere along the coast of South America, when I felt as if I was choking.

Help! I begged, still being pulled.

What?

I scratched at the water, trying to push myself toward air. *I can't breathe! Help!*

I didn't think She took me seriously. After all, how could it be possible? My vision tunneled into nothingness, and I could feel myself slipping away, lungs pressed into angry fists.

Then, with a shift in direction, She took me up. I broke through the surface gasping, lying on Her back as I gagged up water and gulped in air.

Why did you do that? She pressed. *How?*

"I don't know how. I don't know what happened."

What's wrong?

"I needed oxygen." I pushed myself up, legs still resting

on the water, head slumped in exhaustion. "It felt like my lungs were caving in."

That's not possible.

"But that's what happened! I've never felt anything like that."

Shall I call the others back?

"No," I said. "Let me breathe a moment, and I'll catch up to them."

I could feel Her patience waning as I tried to steady my breaths, but it had to be done. Even as I began to feel normal, my heart pounded at the idea of going underwater again. But I knew my job—and all that depended on it—so I dived, hoping to get to the others quickly enough so that they wouldn't be worried.

Where were you? Elizabeth demanded.

Hard to explain. I felt dizzy and sick. I didn't want them to know what had happened.

I was afraid you'd disobeyed. Miaka threw her arms around me.

No. As has been pointed out, that's not my strong suit.

Then what happened?

How could I explain to her, to the others, that I'd stopped being capable of something we all were supposed to be able to do?

Later. For now, let's prepare ourselves.

I'd dodged the peaked rocks as I swam in, so I knew

what was waiting just beneath us. But I doubted the ship in the distance did.

I lay on the water, feeling worn down from losing my breath.

Miaka knelt behind me, and Elizabeth held on to Padma, who muttered to herself, "Not the faces, not the faces, not the faces."

The song filled the empty sky, our voices rising together into the night. I watched the pretty lights of the stars as the ship collided with the rocks on its port side, its speed forcing it sideways.

"Beautiful girl," one man called, swimming to us, his voice joyful. I didn't watch, but his voice grew thicker and thicker with gargled water. "Lov-a-ly!" he sang over and over, until there was eventually nothing left at all.

I waited for the silence, to know we'd gotten each soul, but before their voices gave out, mine did.

I coughed a few times, trying to jump-start my throat to no avail. I moved my mouth with the song, knowing each sound as well as my own heartbeat, but there was only silence. Miaka clutched at my arm, and Elizabeth and Padma shot me concerned looks, but they kept singing.

The moment drew to a close, and I was ashamed to admit how easy it had been for me to forget the people drowning around me. I had been too worried about myself to consider anyone else. I looked back at Padma as she sobbed into Elizabeth's shoulder.

"It's over now. It will get easier each time."

"The screaming is awful," she wept.

Elizabeth's eyes met mine before she bent to Padma's ear. "You did nothing worse than what you did to your father."

"But he deserved it!" she screamed.

The Ocean rumbled beneath us as She yanked us under the surface.

WHAT? She roared.

Padma clung to Elizabeth, and I trembled. All that work for nothing.

I told you no. How could you do this? All Her deadly power and fury was in Her voice.

Because you were wrong! Elizabeth's accusation boomed in our heads. *I walked into Padma's home. I saw how cruel her father was, but now that memory is gone. We destroyed it. None of us could allow her to live in the same world her abusers did. Now they are gone, no one is the wiser, and You still have us at Your beck and call.*

Kahlen, did you know? She sounded hurt at the thought of my betrayal.

I looked around at each of my sisters, wondering what would happen to me now. *Yes. I didn't go, but I made it possible.*

You were to keep them from this!

I could not live with Padma's sorrow. She's been so much better since she came back. Now her second life is real. She's conquered her demons and is Yours completely.

I felt the heat of Her anger stirring around us. Her waves beat at our bodies.

What shall I do with you now?

Sentence us to more time? Elizabeth mocked. *Wouldn't that be smart! Have four rebellious girls trapped at Your side. Or better yet, kill us all! Who would serve You then?*

No, I wouldn't take all of you, the Ocean agreed, something cold and deadly in Her tone. She ripped Padma from Elizabeth's arms, holding her in a vise grip of nothing but water. Padma screamed, trying to move her arms, but was completely paralyzed.

No! I pleaded.

Stop! Elizabeth urged.

Miaka was stunned, her thoughts coming out like a blur of sounds instead of words.

Heed this warning. I cannot take all of you at once, but I can feel your devotion to her. Break My rules again, and she'll pay the price.

Elizabeth's face twisted in anger, waiting for Padma to be restored to us.

Does anyone else have something they'd like to confess?

I wanted to cover Akinli up with other thoughts, worried

about what I might give away. I pushed the memory of my last trip to Port Clyde deep, burying it underneath other, older memories of him.

I miss him, I thought, hoping that would mask my other sins.

I know. She was angry still, but calming.

I hung my head, wishing I was better. I was pegged as the good one, so shouldn't I be?

Very well then. She flung Padma back at Elizabeth, who scooped her into her arms as Miaka rushed to their side. *Get back now, no detours.*

The others moved, but I remained.

How could you? You disobeyed Me again. I could feel Her disappointment.

I felt her pain. It was no way to live. You always said You were giving us our lives back. She never would have had hers as long as she knew they were out there, alive and well, never having paid for what they did.

People are cruel all the time. Not everyone gets what they deserve.

Yet we had an opportunity to give that to someone who might not have had it otherwise. Please don't stay angry. She doesn't need another angry mother.

I felt the Ocean sigh in exasperation.

Why didn't you sing tonight?

I did! Until I couldn't anymore. I have no idea what happened.

This isn't normal. She sounded more irritated than concerned. *You ought to be able to sing and swim. That's what you're made for.*

Am I too old? I know I haven't hit my century yet, but is it possible that whatever is in me is fading?

No. Her voice hardened. *It's much more likely you're being disobedient.*

Why would I do that?

For the same reason you took Padma to her parents. You're angry with Me.

I rolled my eyes. *I miss Akinli. I do. Every day, even when I try not to. But I have Your word to protect him, and I have accepted my fate. By now, You ought to know that I don't disregard You ever for my own sake.*

She considered. The time I didn't sing, pulling Akinli from the water, taking Padma to her parents. None of those things had been solely for me.

True.

Can I go to my sisters? I'm sure Padma is feeling like a piece in a game right now, and I want her to know she is loved.

Yes, She said, Her voice calmer now. *Remind her that she has love. Not only yours, but Mine as well.*

I shook my head. *I can tell her that all I like, but You should prove that to her Yourself. Soon.*

I followed my sisters, worn-out from the evening, and thankful when She pulled me most of the way.

In the house, they were on the couch, Elizabeth and Miaka wrapped around Padma, stroking her hair and shushing her cries.

"She won't kill you," Elizabeth vowed.

"Then why did She say that? There must be some truth to it." Padma shivered in fear.

"She told me to tell you She loves you," I said quietly, feeling more like an observer than a participant in the scene.

Padma shook her head, her face open with hurt.

"I know it doesn't feel that way. It sometimes feels like Her love is torture. But I know it's real. I'm hyperaware of Her attention sometimes, but She has no idea how off the mark She is with how She shows Her love."

I rubbed at my temple, still reeling from the strangeness of the day.

"Kahlen's right," Miaka said, shaking her head. "It's inescapable. But it's so poorly executed that it almost feels like hate."

"Are you excusing what She did today?" Elizabeth demanded.

Miaka stood. "No. Just trying to understand it all myself. How She can take so constantly and be convinced it comes across as affection."

"It's not as if She can practice on an equal." I picked at the salt on my dress, almost feeling sorry for Her.

"I don't want to go back to Her," Padma worried. "I don't want Her to hurt me."

Elizabeth continued to hold her. "She won't. Because we'll be so perfect from here out that She'll never have cause. I promise."

26

When I woke, the sun was low. I had slept a whole day. But I still felt groggy, as if I needed still more sleep. My throat and my chest ached, and I felt hot and dizzy.

"Miaka," I called feebly. "Miaka."

Seconds later, she ran into my room, alerted by the troubled tone in my voice. "What's wrong? Are you okay?"

"I feel weak. I can hardly hold myself up."

She scurried around to my side of the bed, her expression a mixture of worry and confusion, and placed a hand on my forehead.

"Kahlen, you're burning up. How is that possible? You aren't supposed to be able to get sick."

"I know. But this isn't the first time something's gone wrong. Remember the drive back from Florida? And yesterday . . ." I paused on the words, almost embarrassed. "When we were on our way to the ship, I was late because I couldn't breathe. She had to take me to the surface."

"And you couldn't finish the song. I heard you stop singing."

I nodded. "Can you take me to the Ocean?" Despite our disagreements, I yearned for Her to hold me. She could help me, I was sure.

"Hold on, Elizabeth!"

She ran to fetch her. All three of my sisters came into the room whispering, and when Elizabeth's eyes fell on me, they widened in shock.

"You look terrible."

"Help me? Please?" I croaked, my throat dry.

They got under each of my shoulders and pulled me up, Padma walking in front of me and holding her arms out for good measure. I walked on my own, but I knew that if they hadn't been there, I might have fallen more than once. Side by side, we marched into the Ocean, all of us crying for help.

What? I felt the swirling waves of Her worry as we floated just beneath the surface.

Something's wrong with Kahlen, Miaka said.

In the water, they could let me go, and I floated there,

263

the Ocean holding me like a child.

I'm so tired.

Look at her skin, Elizabeth said. *She's so pale. And she keeps sleeping. Like she needs it.*

She has a fever, too, Miaka added. I was acutely aware that my temperature was off; I could feel the water around me warming from my touch.

Padma had bravely come into the water with us but stayed behind Elizabeth as if she could hide. Miaka's eyes were careful, observant, but the others couldn't mask their worry.

The Ocean examined me, lifting my arms and asking me to blink my eyes.

So, not disobedience?

No, I thought. *I can't control it.*

She fretted. *This has never happened before. I don't know what to do.*

Maybe if she stays in You for a while, it would help, Elizabeth suggested.

What, Miaka? the Ocean asked suddenly.

Nothing. But she did look like she was hiding something.

What were you thinking?

Nothing, Miaka insisted. *Flipping through ideas, it's all nothing. I think Elizabeth is onto something.* She swam up to me. *We'll come and check on you every hour until you feel like coming back to bed.*

I didn't want to say how much it bothered me that she said "back to bed" instead of "back to the house." It was like she knew I wasn't going to be standing again.

Okay.

They fled, off to make arrangements for their broken sister.

I'm sorry. I don't know what's happening.

How long have you been feeling like this? She sounded uneasy, as if She suspected something She didn't want to say.

I squinted, trying to remember. *It's been coming on so slowly, it's hard to say.*

She snuggled me into Herself. *Just rest. I'm here.*

And I was so tired, I did exactly that. It was so unreal, how loved I felt. Right there, balanced with Her rigidity, Her absolute need to maintain order, I heard Her thinking of what She might sacrifice so long as She could keep me. It was such an encompassing feeling, and that alone was enough to make me sleep.

I was woken by Miaka rubbing my shoulder. *Hey. We thought you should get some food. If your energy is waning, maybe that will help. Humans need it.*

But I'm not human.

She smiled. *Sure you are. Underneath it all.*

Maybe also warmth, She added. *I'll expect updates.*

Of course. Padma's too afraid to come on her own, so it will probably be Elizabeth.

All right. But don't wait too long.

We won't. Miaka put an arm under me and pulled me home.

"Feeling any better?" she asked as we slowly made our way up the slope to the house.

"I don't feel worse. But I'm certainly not indestructible right now."

"You won't die. It's not possible."

"Which has been the theme of my life lately. And yet."

Miaka was quiet as she took me inside, and Elizabeth was in the kitchen, apron around her waist as she ladled broth into a bowl. "Hi!" she greeted overenthusiastically. "I made chicken noodle soup. It's supposed to be a cure-all."

They put me in soft leggings and an oversize sweater that still had the tag on it before sitting me on the couch. A small tray was placed in front of me, and while I had no desire to eat, the fear in their faces drove me to spoon the noodles and carrots and spices into my mouth. I couldn't take too much, but then again, I wasn't designed for food.

When I turned the rest of it away, they exchanged looks.

"I think it's time to tell her," Miaka said. "She needs to know the whole story."

"What story?" I asked, wondering what they'd kept from me.

"I didn't tell them," she vowed, sitting across from me on an ottoman. "They figured it out on their own."

I squinted. "Figured out what?"

Elizabeth reached into her back pocket and pulled out a sheet of paper. "About him."

I felt faint as I stared into Akinli's eyes. "Where did you get that?"

"From you. You drew it and threw it away, remember?"

I closed my eyes. I remembered. "It's just a drawing. A very bad one. Nothing like Miaka's."

Elizabeth shook her head. "He's much more than a drawing. I've seen him."

I was aghast. "What do you mean?"

"You drew this picture. You said you were in a small town, Port Clyde. All you have ever wanted was to fall in love, and you were so deeply depressed when you came back, I knew. Miaka only confirmed it."

"How . . . I tried so hard. . . ." I was having trouble thinking, I was so shocked.

"When we were in New York, you cried for two days and passed out. You said a word in your sleep, over and over. Akinli." Elizabeth stared down at the drawing.

"At first I thought it was gibberish. And then I thought it was the name of a town or a building. . . . I didn't figure

267

out it belonged to a person until you made that." Elizabeth pointed down to the paper, worn from being folded and unfolded who knew how many times.

"When Elizabeth came to me, I had to tell her the truth, and we decided to find him. You gave us the name of the town. We went there looking for someone answering to that name, fitting this image." Miaka smiled ruefully. "Very small town. It wasn't hard."

Tears pooled in my eyes. "You've really seen him?"

They both nodded. I thought about all those trips they had taken, making up ridiculous stories so they could get to him without me knowing.

"How is he?" I asked, unable to contain my curiosity. "Is he okay? Has he gone back to school? Is he still with Ben and Julie? Is he happy? Could you tell? Is he happy?"

The questions tumbled out without me being able to hold them in. I was desperate to know. I felt a single word would put my soul at ease.

Elizabeth swallowed hard. "That's the thing, Kahlen. We're afraid he's dying."

They told the Ocean I'd eaten, omitting the fact that it all came back up. They told Her I was still awake, leaving out that it was because I couldn't stop crying. These half-truths would keep Her pacified for now, though I knew

She'd find out soon that I was feeling worse than I'd imagined possible.

"How can you know he's dying?" I asked. "It doesn't make sense; he was so healthy. Is it cancer?"

That seemed the only option, a quiet killer that pounced even on the strongest of humans, taking them down without them knowing what was coming.

Miaka shook her head. "He's been tested. He's been looked at for a number of things."

"How in the world could you know this?"

"By following him to the doctor and sitting in the waiting room. By listening to his cousin update friends on the dock. By scheduling a makeover appointment with Julie, who I think misses you, by the way."

"Really?" My aching paused for a moment as I tried to wrap my head around that.

"I had to pretend to be deaf, of course, and I hadn't expected her to speak at all. But she talked to herself about how I was just like this pretty girl she knew, this girl who didn't speak. She told me how nice it had been to have another girl around, how she was worried you'd drowned."

I sighed. "So that's what they think happened to me. Makes sense."

"But here's the thing, Kahlen. His symptoms are similar to yours. He's weak and pale. He's in a wheelchair."

I covered my mouth.

"He's covered in bruises because everything hurts him. Sleeping, sitting, moving at all. The doctors don't know what to do."

"So . . . we're sick."

"Yes. I don't know how it's possible that you both have the same disease, especially when you shouldn't be able to catch it at all. But I'm doing research. If we can find a name for it, maybe we can find someone who knows how to treat it."

"Miaka . . . will he die from this?"

She shrugged helplessly. "I don't know. I've never studied medicine. But he looks like he's deteriorating. It must be because you're a siren that you've been mostly fine until now. From what I've picked up, he seems to have been suffering from this since about three months after you parted."

I nodded, trying to imagine Akinli in a wheelchair, inexplicably ill for almost a year.

"Is it communicable then? Did I catch this from him?"

She shrugged. "That's our best guess. So I'm researching now."

"Can I help?"

She tilted her head lovingly. "We need you to rest. We need you to be as strong as you can be so that when we find a cure, you'll be ready."

"How do you know you'll even find a cure?"

She stared at me, her eyes intent. "Kahlen, I pity anyone who stands between me and an antidote. Because I'm deadly. And for the first time ever, I think I'd have the Ocean's approval if I needed to take out someone who got in our way."

I swallowed. She was probably right.

"Take me to Her. Let me rest there. It'll be better for you all if I'm out of the way."

It was Elizabeth who walked me down, as Miaka was the one making the most headway research wise.

"Listen, Kahlen. We're going to figure this out."

"I know. I trust you."

Elizabeth grimaced. "Sorry we didn't tell you where we disappeared to. At first we hoped we'd be able to find him and tell you how he was, make you happier. Then when we saw how badly he was doing, we wanted to wait until he was better. And then . . ."

"Then you saw he wasn't getting better."

She nodded. "I'm sorry."

We stopped just before the water, and she held on to me. I was too tired to cry. "I know it shouldn't hurt," I said. "Because he never really could have been mine anyway, and I know that every life ends, and it isn't the amount of time we have that makes it valuable. It's still just heartbreaking. All I wanted was his happiness."

"That makes it worse for us. Because all we want is yours, and it hangs on his."

I took a deep, sobbing breath. "Life is pointless. Love is pointless. And still, wouldn't I do every second of it all over again?"

"I'm guessing yes."

"Undoubtedly. Yes. Yes every time."

She smiled at me, at our fruitless lives, and helped me down.

I've been waiting for news! Is it a disease? The Ocean demanded the second Elizabeth's feet hit the surf.

"Miaka's researching. There isn't much to say yet," she began.

"That's not true." I turned to my sister. "Leave us alone. Let me tell Her what we know. Everything."

Elizabeth huffed. "If you want." And she left me in the water as gently as she could while still being quick.

I knew she was worried for herself, for Padma, but this wasn't time for secret keeping.

I'm catching pieces of your thoughts, but they're very scattered.

Sorry. My body gave an involuntary shiver. *I'm still trying to line them all up.*

Start with New York. That's what I see.

I braced myself. *I told Miaka about Akinli and what happened in Port Clyde. I thought I'd hidden it from the others, but apparently I said his name in my sleep, I drew a picture of him without thinking about it, and I told them the name of the town. They knew he was the source of my sadness and set out to pass along news about him.*

Ah. So I've been living with more lies than I knew. Her voice was heavy with disapproval.

Yes. But You might be glad for these lies.

How so?

Whatever I have, Akinli has as well, I informed Her. *So there's at least one more case.*

There was a long, heavy pause. *That's impossible.*

He has the same symptoms as I do. Meaning we have a place to start. If he passed it on to me, we know that it's communicable and that it's strong. We also know doctors are looking for answers. Miaka is hunting for other cases, seeing if we can find an origin. Their lies might keep me alive.

She sighed in relief. *Your sisters care for you, although I believe they are mistaken. I will forget their disobedience.*

Thank you. My body felt heavy, like it might sink to the sand any second.

Is there anything you need?

Sleep.

Of course. The Ocean made Herself into a bed, putting tension under my body so I could get comfortable.

I tried to let myself rest, but even as tired as I was, sleep evaded me. For so long, I'd felt my life was out of my control. Now it was in the truest way possible. This wasn't about freedom or choices; this was about survival. And I could do nothing about it.

I hated being disconnected from the search, more for Akinli's pain than mine. Nearly a year of this. How much longer could he endure? If *my* body was failing, how could—

I gagged on the water. Then, in trying to draw breath, I choked on more. With the little energy I had, I tried to swim to the surface. But without words, the Ocean was aware of my struggle and pushed me to air.

Miaka! Elizabeth! Padma!

I lay on top of the water, throwing up water and the small bits of food they'd been trying to get me to eat. No more of that.

I was close enough to the house that I could see them running. When they hit the Ocean, She solidified for them so they could run across Her back to me.

"Kahlen?" Padma cried.

"She's breathing!" Elizabeth's words were echoing in my ears.

Carry her back. She cannot go in My waters. She can't breathe.

Padma sucked in a breath. "Oh, no."

"It's worse than I thought," Miaka whispered.

I'd have told her I could still hear her, but it took too much work to speak.

They lifted me effortlessly, carrying me across the edge

of the Pacific, taking me into the house. I recognized the heat of the shower, the comfort of clean clothes, and the tender way Padma tucked me in, but I was so exhausted, so frightened, I couldn't even say thank-you.

27

By the next day, I was able to sit up in bed. I could tell that I'd be able to walk if I needed to, but I had no desire to move from my spot. It was safe and warm, though I took little comfort in it. I was deeply aware of that string tied to Akinli. And now, more than ever, I felt the tension between our bodies, split across the country, sharing a similar ache.

Maybe it was something that had been there the whole time, or maybe it had only emerged once I'd decided to sneak back to Port Clyde, but there were moments when I felt something akin to the pulse after touching a bruise, and I was certain it was his weakness echoing in me.

Weeks passed, and events swirled around me. While I

lay in bed, conserving what energy I had, the Ocean was intentionally tracking news. She listened to the thoughts of every soul who swam in a lake or basked with their toes in the surf. As fishermen plunged their hands into water or lovers flirted with their feet off a dock, She was there. No one spoke of a mysterious new epidemic robbing people of their vitality, crippling bodies.

I'm looking, She vowed, Her voice coming in through the walls. *I'm searching for answers.*

It was pitiable that I could not answer Her, and I could hear the unimaginable worry of the Ocean, agonizing that I, Her eldest, was fading.

And yet, I still felt that She was holding something back. There was a heaviness in Her voice, as if She suspected something She didn't want to believe. I was afraid to ask Her. What if what She knew was that there was no cure?

Miaka forced me onto a scale for the third time in a week. "That's another two pounds. How are you losing weight?"

"Please don't make me try to eat again."

She scooped me up, and I wondered at how waifish I must be becoming if she carried me so effortlessly.

"What if it was all drinkable? Plenty of patients have to resort to liquid diets."

Patients? There were many words I didn't like to use to define myself. *Murderer, fictional, soulless. Patient* was going on that list.

"How do you know?" I asked, leaning my head into her neck as we turned down the hall.

"Because I've been parked in front of a computer for the last month trying to find out what's wrong with you."

She tucked me back into bed. The house was strangely quiet. I'd grown used to Elizabeth's exasperated huffs and Padma's quiet snuffles. They took their turn in searching as well, but they weren't as driven as Miaka. "Where are the others?"

"Checking on Akinli." Padma wasn't mature enough to go out on her own, but she had happily joined Elizabeth and Miaka in monitoring his health.

I felt a little lift in my pulse. "Really?"

"Yes. And with the Ocean's consent. I've been hunting everywhere. Checking the CDC for clues, watching chatter online, and even looking in Third World countries for anything that might resemble what's happening to you two. So far, nothing. The others are going to find out how he's doing and, if possible, try to get to his medical records."

"They could go to jail."

She shrugged. "They could get out of jail."

I let out a single laugh, my lips feeling taut from the strain. "Probably."

"We need to know his diagnosis if possible. It's a long shot, but that might help us know how to treat you."

"Even if how he's being treated isn't helping him?"

She sighed. "We're going to figure this out for both of you."

Miaka brushed my hair back from my face, a tender gesture that melted my heart. I had been so glad when she came into the sisterhood. I knew now that the Ocean didn't have much of a method in choosing Her sirens, but when Miaka joined us, I had thought that she was a present for me. She made losing Marilyn so much easier, and her then quiet nature was perfect for me. She kept me together for so, so long.

"Kahlen, would you please consider the liquid diet? I feel like getting some calories into you might do a world of good."

I hated not to let her try whatever she wanted to help me, but I knew my face gave away my skepticism. "I'm a siren. Above human, above girl. Whatever is wrong with me or Akinli, a human need like food won't be the cure."

Miaka inhaled to chastise me, concern written across her face, when she froze.

"Oh . . . why didn't I think of that!"

"Of what?"

Her eyes lit up with excitement, and she covered her mouth as the gears in her brain started turning. "We've been going about this backward. You're right. You're a siren. We assumed that Akinli made you sick, so we were looking for an illness, a disease. But maybe it started with you!"

"With me?"

"Yes! What if we need to treat him for something that could hurt sirens? What if, in curing that, we cure you?"

I stared at nothing, trying first to get over the guilt at possibly causing Akinli's brokenness, then trying to fathom what this could mean.

"Miaka . . . that's brilliant. But there's only one problem."

"What?"

"What hurts sirens?"

Her shoulders slumped. "Good point." Miaka drummed her fingers across her chin. "I need to talk to the Ocean. She *must* know. She's had so many of us serve Her. If there's an illness that affects sirens . . . Will you be all right by yourself for a bit?"

"Sure."

She took off, an urgent need for answers pushing her forward.

I let out a long breath, cursing myself for perhaps having any part in hurting Akinli. Of course I valued my life; I had so many hopes for it. But when I held it up next to his, thinking of all the hurt I'd caused so many people—not just by ending their lives but by forcing their loved ones to go on without them—I hoped if only one of us could be saved, it might be him.

So far my existence had only brought sorrow. His had the potential to bring so much joy.

I closed my eyes, fixing Akinli in the forefront of my thoughts. *I'm so sorry*, I said to the last image I had of him, the healthy, happy boy kissing me on the beach.

And almost instantly, I felt a pulse of affection go through me, and it was as if Akinli were near me, as if we could wrap our arms around each other. With that comfort, I drifted off to sleep again.

"Undiagnosed." Elizabeth threw the waterlogged copies of Akinli's medical records on the table. "They tested for cancer, liver failure, thyroid disorders, the whole gamut. They even looked into depression and grief, which were definite possibilities since his parents are gone and even more so if he misses you the way you miss him."

I sat, covered in blankets at the table, looking at the stack of papers. "How are they paying for all this?" I worried aloud.

Elizabeth rolled her eyes. "Of course that's where your head goes. Don't worry. We'll set up an anonymous donation."

I nodded. At least we could do that. "Did you see him?" I asked, trying not to sound too eager. Secretly, I wished they'd heard him speak of me or something, though I knew it was unlikely. "Is he looking any better?"

Padma stared down at the ground guiltily, as if she was ashamed. Reaching into her pocket, she pulled out a handful of pictures. I took them from her, both eager and anxious.

I recognized the blue eyes, the scruffy blond hair that peeked from underneath the knit hat he clearly needed for warmth now. But the curves of his cheeks had turned to angles, the light in his face to a dim glow, still alight but barely.

"Oh, no," I gasped, covering my mouth, hot tears coming to my eyes. "Akinli, no."

The pictures, obviously taken from the forest across from his house, showed that Ben and Julie had put in a wheelchair ramp, new and crisp, which looked all wrong against the rest of their beautifully timeworn home.

"They were taking him for a walk. It's really remarkable, Kahlen." I squinted up at Elizabeth, confused. What could be so fascinating about the fact that the boy I loved could no longer walk? "Even like this, everyone he saw was so thrilled to have him come by. This old woman with a mess of a front yard . . ."

"Ms. Jenkens," I said with a smile.

"Yeah." She smirked, seeming unsurprised that I knew. "She put a tray of cookies in his lap. He ate one or two but gave the rest to the kids hanging out near the dock. We got pretty close." She pointed back to the pictures, and I flipped to the others. "He was telling the kids not to let it get back to her that he'd given the cookies away. He didn't want to hurt her feelings."

I shook my head. "So him."

"While you were gone," Miaka began, all business, "we think we had a breakthrough. I'm not surprised his records say nothing, because we're starting to think this isn't something medical. It's mythical."

Padma and Elizabeth exchanged a confused glance.

"We've been trying to treat Kahlen for a human condition when she's not human, and it's getting us nowhere. We're starting to think he didn't pass something on to her; she passed something on to him."

"Oh!" Elizabeth said, both intrigued and confused. "But what? How?"

"That's the question. I asked the Ocean, but She didn't have an answer for me. She said this has never happened before. So now we're shifting focus. We're not looking for a human diagnosis; we're looking at siren history. Somewhere there must be a hint at what could simultaneously kill a human and siren while causing nothing to happen to those around them or to the Ocean Herself."

Padma was nodding. "I will help, but I know so little next to you."

"Don't worry," Miaka began. "At the moment, we all know nothing."

I was ushered back to bed while Elizabeth drove to town to fetch books from the library, and Miaka went back to scouring the internet for leads.

No one noticed that I held on to the pictures, and I set up the one with the closest shot of Akinli's face against my lamp.

We'll figure this out, I promised. *I won't let you sink.*

I stared into his tired eyes, still seeing the beauty in him. Whatever happened, I'd met my person, the one my soul connected to, despite age and distance and impossibility. I stared at the photo as if he and I were settling down for a nap, side by side, and I swore I could hear Akinli's voice saying *Hurry*.

28

Miaka scrutinized all the paintings of sirens she could find, spanning across human history to collect them. She blew up several, tacking them to the wall. In a notebook, she analyzed color usage, symbolism, historical context. She hunted down patrons if she could, finding out if someone had commissioned a piece or if it had been born of the artist's inspiration alone.

I wasn't sure for a long time why she did this, how art could help us now.

"Maybe someone actually saw one of us," she tried to explain. "Maybe it was an accident or a survivor She'd missed. Maybe there's a record . . . I don't know. I'll take anything."

Elizabeth found references to us in a few movies and watched them repeatedly, looking to see if there were similar themes among them. For me, that seemed as pointless now as it had when I tried my hand at researching sirens myself. But Elizabeth was no scholar. She was a fighter. In the absence of someone to fight, this was the best she could do.

And Padma. Sweet Padma set herself to reading every myth, every fable, every fairy tale. It was a fact that too many people ignored: Children's books held truths.

During my previous research on sirens, I'd kept my studies secret. I had been reluctant to have my sisters know I was looking for an escape route. But maybe I should have said something. Seeing us now, huddled together, learning things the Ocean could never teach us about ourselves . . . I felt closer to them than I had in a long time, and I wanted to cry, thinking I might have only truly fallen in love with my sisters on the edge of my death.

And with them, I discovered much more than I had alone. We read about the Slavic *rusalki*, who were the souls of women who drowned and haunted rivers and streams. The Latin undines lacked a soul but could obtain one through marriage to a mortal. Mermaids had their long hair and beautiful tails, naiads only lived in freshwater, and the Greeks had a slew of gods dedicated to nothing but water. Still, no matter how far we wandered down these trails, wondering if maybe one of these myths had been inspired by us, we didn't find anything that might explain my sickness.

Between fits of sleep that I couldn't fight off, I read. At first, I found this all as frustrating as I had in the past. There were pieces of things we knew to be true. The numbers, the song, the inevitable death. But the rest seemed to be fiction, things dreamed up by men to paint us as heartless women who lived to seduce them, even in the myths about other water creatures. All women, all intent on destruction.

But I had a heart. I had a heart, and it was breaking.

It was in the middle of all this that I picked up a collection of short stories. I recognized the title although I'd never read it before. This book had come out about the time I'd been changed. I flipped to the piece by Franz Kafka called "The Silence of the Sirens." It was barely two pages long . . . yet I couldn't stop thinking about his words, the idea that a siren's silence was more deadly than her song.

I scoffed at it initially, but I couldn't shake it off. How could my silence be deadly? My silence was the only thing keeping people alive. I finished the story and moved on to other things, but that thought came back to me over and over, though I wasn't sure why.

My silence hadn't killed anyone. If our not singing was

so deadly, then anyone we came into contact with should be experiencing what Akinli was.

I considered every other tie I had to him, worrying I wasn't moving fast enough to help. It wasn't that we'd kissed, I knew that. Elizabeth had kissed more than her share of human men without the slightest ill effect. It wasn't that I loved him, because if love could kill, then Aisling never would have made it back to Tova, to her great-grandchild. So what was it? What was setting Akinli apart from everyone else?

"Miaka," I called, my voice so hoarse I wondered if my song would even work right now.

"What? Are you hungry? Do you feel sick?" she questioned, abandoning everything for me.

"Can you read this for me? It's short, but something about it . . . ." I passed the thin book up to her, and she studied it briefly. "Anything jump out at you?"

She took it from my frail hands, reading through the passage in a fraction of the time I had.

"How could our silence be more deadly than our song?" she sneered.

"Exactly."

She handed back the book. "I'll keep thinking about it."

"Any luck with the art?"

She huffed. "No. Mostly it seems like we're demonized or sexualized."

288

"I noticed."

"And as far as I can tell, no one has knowingly seen a siren and lived to tell the tale."

"Someone must have," I croaked, wrapping my blankets even tighter around myself. "Otherwise how would anyone even have a place to start the myth?"

"Well, whoever that person was, they've been dead for thousands of years and left little more than we already know."

I sighed. My head was already worn-out from the day, and I could feel my heart fading right behind it.

Miaka put her hands on my shoulders, and the warmth was welcome, except that it made me aware of how cold I was. "We'll crack this, Kahlen. I feel like we're so close."

I nodded, though I wasn't sure I agreed. I was worried Akinli was running out of time, his fragile body much more breakable than mine. And I couldn't help but wonder, since our sickness was linked, what would happen to my heart if his stopped beating?

Elizabeth marched over from the living room. "Pointless. I'm not a man-eater," she said, flicking her head toward the television.

"Well, if any one of us could be . . . ," Miaka began, her tone joking.

Elizabeth gave the hint of a smile, and it helped me just to feel like we could tease each other right now.

I gave the biggest grin I could, which didn't amount to much, and felt a tiny, sharp pain at the corner of my mouth. I touched my hand to it, hoping to dull the sting. When I pulled back my hand, the tips of my fingers were bright red.

I stared at the blood, horrified. I'd been taken off guard by the nausea and fevers, and shocked by the exhaustion and aches. But this made me look my mortality square in the face. I still thought I was above bleeding.

The girls exchanged nervous glances, not knowing what to say or do. Padma got a towel from the kitchen and cleaned my hand and lip for me as we all dealt with this new blow in silence.

"What aren't we seeing?" Elizabeth asked desperately. "What don't we know? We've seen every film, looked at every painting, read every book. . . . Don't we know every story by now?"

"Well, no," Padma said as if what we'd skipped was obvious. "I don't know hers." She pointed to me.

"I was changed the same as you," I began with a shrug. "It was nineteen—"

"No, no." Padma laughed. "I mean with this boy. What exactly happened between you? How did you even meet?"

"In Florida. He worked at the library. We met a couple of times. The last time, we got together and made a cake."

"Then you lost contact?"

I lowered my eyes. "I liked him too much. When I

realized I was falling in love with him, I knew I had to leave for both our sakes."

"And?"

"I dragged the girls from Miami to Pawleys Island. We hadn't been there for very long when you came to us." I stopped to take a breath. It was getting harder to breathe. "I thought that I was doing okay, but you saw what happened when we were singing and She took down a cruise ship with a wedding party on board. I couldn't handle it. All I ever wanted was to be that bride, and to take her life on the very day she got what I longed for   it was too much. So I left Her, and ended up in Port Clyde, where Akinli lived. It felt like I was pulled there by something deep inside me. I didn't expect him to be there or to find me right out of the water."

"You weren't there with him long at all," Padma leaned in, resting her head on her hand, taking in everything. I realized then that Miaka had gotten her notebook and was writing down all this.

"A day. Barely over twenty-four hours."

"Okay," Miaka began, "outline everything. He took you to his house?"

I told her again about Ben and Julie, how they had opened their home to me. I told them about Akinli making me breakfast, and how I'd learned we each almost died with our parents.

"Could that be it?" Elizabeth asked. "That's a strange thing to have in common."

"I don't think so, but I'll make a note," Miaka said. "What next?"

I told them about the bookstore, the story in sign language, and the ice cream.

"Did you share a spoon or anything?" Padma asked. "Would that spread some of that liquid She puts in us?"

Miaka shook her head. "I'll write it down, but it's unlikely. If it were that simple, Elizabeth would have killed dozens of men by now."

"Not dozens!" she protested. "But, yes, I've shared plenty of . . . fluids with human men. And others have done that before us. Nothing like this has come of it."

"How could you be sure?" I asked. "It's not like any of us have had a long enough relationship to be able to tell."

"I . . . ," Elizabeth stammered. "There was one I thought was particularly charming. I went back to him once. It was several months after the first time, and he was in perfect health."

"All right. Documented. You know," Miaka stated hesitantly, "the Ocean will want to know about all this."

Elizabeth actually growled considering that.

"All right. What else?"

I talked about the brief afternoon at his house, how Julie was grateful I came. And then our date.

"So how did you leave this time?"

I had to pause. It was almost as painful as this consuming sickness to think about.

"He took me to his house. Not Ben's, but his parents' house. He knew. . . . I don't know how he pieced it all together, but he knew there was something off about me. Instead of being afraid, he offered to protect me. He asked me to stay, and suddenly I thought maybe I could do it. We lived among humans all the time, so how would this be any different?" I blinked, and the tears streamed onto my cheeks. "And then he kissed me. That's all. Just a perfect, timeless kiss. And in a complete moment of stupidity, I said, 'Wow.'"

I shook my head. "His eyes went funny, and he headed for the Ocean. I tried to stop him, but he just went deeper and deeper. I pleaded with Her, promising to bring others in his place. It's so shameful to admit, but I think I would have if She'd asked. Anything to keep him alive." I wiped at the tears, embarrassed at how quickly I would have turned on others if it meant he was safe.

"She let him live. . . . I wasn't supposed to tell you, but She let him live. I got him to land, kissed him, and went back to the Ocean.

"I haven't seen him since."

"Huh," Padma said. "So . . . nothing too crazy, just a mistake."

I nodded.

"Wait . . . what was that you were saying about silence?" Elizabeth asked. "Weren't you talking about some quote just before I came over?"

"This book was saying that a siren's silence is more deadly than her song, which sounds crazy if you—"

She held up a hand to silence me. "What if that's it?"

"What?"

"Your silence." She seemed incredibly excited, but I squinted, not following. "He might be the only person on the planet who has heard the voice of a siren and lived. What if that's what's killing him? Your silence?"

"But I couldn't keep speaking to him," I protested. "That would surely kill him as well."

"Even if you're right," Miaka objected, gripping her notebook, "it wouldn't explain why Kahlen's getting sick now. This might mean nothing."

Elizabeth shrugged. "But it's our first real clue."

29

I knew with a cold horror that Akinli was dying, that his end was near. The same odd connection that told me he was in Port Clyde and not Miami, that brought a strange sense of peace sometimes, made me sure of it.

I squeezed my eyes shut, but there was nothing left to cry out. My body shook with dry sobs. If I was going to save Akinli, I needed to hurry. The string holding our lives aloft, tying our souls to each other, was about to snap. I didn't know if his life ending meant mine would as well, but I was sure that if my impenetrable body could founder this much, death would come eventually.

"I still don't understand," I rasped. "If our voices make people drown themselves, why would my silence be what's killing Akinli?"

Miaka rubbed at her eyes, thinking, thinking, thinking. "I don't know. How does any of this work?"

"Maybe there's a place to start. Ask the Ocean about our voice, about the song." Elizabeth shrugged, looking as frustrated as Miaka.

"Come with me?" Miaka pleaded with Elizabeth. "You were the one who thought that following this trail might find something. Maybe you'll ask a question I'd never think of."

Elizabeth nodded. "Of course. You need anything?" She turned to me.

"No. If I do, I have Padma."

Padma leaned into me. "Always."

"We'll be fine."

I watched Elizabeth and Miaka walk away, clutching at each other's hands.

This was all my fault. All I'd ever meant to do was follow the rules, and this was what I got for breaking them. My sisters were worried sick, I could no longer be with the Ocean, and Akinli was dying. All because of me.

"Sorry I dragged you into this, Padma. I swear—life isn't usually this eventful." I gave a weak chuckle and wiped at where my tears should have been.

"I don't mind. It's been nice to feel like there's a purpose to what I'm doing. I know I have a role for the Ocean, and I have a role among my sisters. It's satisfying. The real question is, what will I do all day once you're well again?"

"I appreciate your optimism."

She pressed her lips together. "I'm trying. I was difficult when you found me. I have a lot to let go of. Plenty is gone, and you helped me find some peace, but there are other things about myself I have to relearn."

"Like?" I pulled some of my blanket across her, and she cuddled under it with me.

"That I am capable of doing a real job. That I am not a burden. That I deserve a chance at life just as much as anyone else. That it is possible to love me."

I held her hand. "Oh, Padma, it's not just possible, it's inevitable. You're precious to us, and to the Ocean, too."

"I know. Frightened as She makes me, I feel love underneath Her aggression."

Despite the rage I felt at the Ocean because of the role I had to play for Her, I knew that She would treasure Padma as She treasured us all. "Give Her time, and She will be like the mother you should have had."

"Our voices are poison," Miaka said.

"Poison?"

"Yes. Our effect on humans is twofold. First, the song lures them to death. And second, our voices are toxic. I think that's what's happened here. The remnants of your voice are deteriorating Akinli's body, and since sound isn't like a pill or liquid, I don't think the doctors know what to look for."

I nodded. "Okay, poison. What about the song?"

Elizabeth wrapped her arms around herself. "It makes sense now that it's all in sounds we slightly recognize but don't fully understand. The song has a little bit of every language in it. The Ocean told me what the words mean. It's actually kind of heartbreaking."

Miaka said the lyrics, a slight lilt in her voice echoing the familiar melody, though the syllables didn't quite match up.

> *"Come throw your heart into the waves*
> *Your soul is lost, and still it saves*
> *Drink me in and come undone*
> *Trade a thousand lives for one*
> *Come away, drink it in*
> *Drink and sink and let it end*
> *Drink and sink and let it end*
> *You are no more, you are no less*
> *For all must die, all must rest*
> *Bring your body unto me*
> *Let your graveyard be the sea*
> *Come away and drink it in*
> *Drink and sink and let it end*
> *Drink and sink and let it end"*

We were silent afterward, taking in the meaning of the sounds we'd always made. I'd thought several times that it was a lovely mix of languages, and now I felt sure that was so everyone, regardless of their origin, would understand the call to die.

I shivered. "It's a lullaby for a death march."

"But there's a promise in it, and it's all so beautifully seductive. 'Trade a thousand lives for one.' Meaning your death provides for the masses. It's hauntingly poetic." I could tell Miaka was battling with herself, repulsed by the song and admiring it at the same time.

"So what does this mean? Does it give us any hope for saving Akinli?"

Miaka bit her lip. "I don't know. It seems like we're missing something. Our voices are toxic, and the song we sing lures people to their death. You didn't sing the song to Akinli—maybe that's why he's still alive—but none of what we've found out explains why you're sick, too."

Padma frowned. "What else did the Ocean say?"

"When She explained how our voices work, it seemed like She accepted why Akinli was sick," Elizabeth said. "But when we asked Her about Kahlen, She just said that it was impossible."

I blinked. "She said the same thing to me," I said, remembering. There had been something strange in Her voice, though, hadn't there? A heaviness and hesitation, a tone that didn't mean the issue was truly impossible, but that it was something the speaker refused to believe.

My whole body felt raw and achy, and when I tried to get up, the room swung nauseatingly around me and I had to drop back onto my pillows, panting.

"Stop," Elizabeth said sharply. "What are you trying to do?"

I reached out for my sisters. "Take me to the Ocean," I begged them. "Please."

30

It was with extreme care that I was lifted from my bed, carried on a blanket by my sisters down to the Ocean. I shivered in the nearly arctic air, thinking that, if things hadn't been so dire recently, I'd have asked to move somewhere warmer, someplace where my fading body might fare better.

We were out of time. My sisters had told me that Akinli was now unable to leave his room, and it felt as if I wasn't too far off from being in the same predicament. My only hope was that, if the Ocean genuinely felt how close I was to death, She would tell us the secret that She was hiding. If in fact She did know something She wasn't sharing with us.

I knew that I was Her only concern at the moment.

Akinli would be the collateral damage of my mistake, but so long as I was brought back, it didn't matter to Her what happened to him. And She would know soon, if She hadn't guessed already, that if I was saved, I'd find a way to share it with Akinli. I was far too tired to hold anything back now.

"Ah!" I squealed when my legs were dipped into the water. "It's like knives in my skin!"

Wait.

We stood by the surf, still and confused. How were we going to manage this?

Here. Try again.

My feet went in, surprised to find the water now luke-warm.

This should be more comfortable.

"Should the rest of us get in?" Padma asked.

"Why don't you two go?" Miaka suggested. "I'll keep Kahlen upright."

There were no words at first. Only a sense of worry as the Ocean channeled Padma's and Elizabeth's thoughts through Her own.

I didn't realize you had gotten so much worse. You haven't come to Me for a while. The Ocean sounded . . . frightened?

I leaned into Miaka, my chest jolting up in tiny flutters like a bird. "I'm going to die," I told Her. "It's worse now."

"You won't die," Miaka promised. "There has to be

302

something we just can't see."

Ah.

I could feel Her going through my thoughts, all my memories of Akinli as they came to the surface. Most of everything before I was changed had fallen into darkness now, and this life was so long there weren't many seasons of it that felt worth remembering. But Akinli . . . everything with him was crystal clear.

She felt how endearing I'd found his attempts to speak to me in the library, how my heart had lifted when he danced with me by the tree. She saw his line of texts on my long-lost phone, how my mind had flitted back to him over and over the first time we were separated. She felt how welcomed I'd been when he took me to his house, how warm it had been when he pressed his side against mine in the bookstore. She felt how magical my first kiss was. Heaven help me, even now that kiss felt like a beautiful thing, a wonder that should be placed under a glass box and marveled at by the masses.

And, because I genuinely could not hold it back, She saw how I missed him. I felt Her recoil at the sadness I'd been fighting for my sisters' sake, for Hers.

Until she pulled in a jagged breath, I didn't know Miaka was crying. She shook her head, covering her mouth, the fingers she held against my back digging sharply into me for support.

"Miaka?"

"I'm sorry. All this time I blamed you for not snapping out of whatever was bringing you down. And now that I feel it . . . Kahlen, you did better than I would have. It's so heavy."

Padma flung herself onto the rocks, coming out of the water as if she were running from a monster. She fell to her knees ten feet away from us, sobbing uncontrollably. Elizabeth came out, too, though slower, trudging through the last steps to the shore.

"We'll go back," she said. "Neither of us could take it, and we just need a break until the thoughts shift. I don't know if your feelings for Akinli really go that deep or if the Ocean amplifies them, but damn."

No. Those are hers.

Elizabeth nodded, looking too dejected to do much more. "Can she just go back to him?" she pleaded. "He's dying. She's dying. They can't have a life together, but at least they could have this."

No, Kahlen is Mine. We'll fix her.

"With what?" Elizabeth demanded through tears. "There's nothing left."

"Please," I said, letting all the dams burst, exposing every last drop of love I had for Akinli. "You've seen how I feel now. I've shared everything . . . but I'm sensing that You haven't."

I could feel several things as Her thoughts processed. Guilt, disbelief, worry, shame. And with that I knew She'd been keeping secrets.

"Please. What aren't You telling me?"

It's impossible, She insisted, and again I heard the strangeness in Her voice. *I never doubted your ability to love, but what mortal could truly love a girl who he knew for so little time? How could he see past the beauty I have given you to your true self, especially when you could not speak with him?*

"What do You mean?" Miaka said, tensing. "Have You known what's been wrong with Kahlen this whole time?"

"Please," I said again, "I love You. You've always treasured me. Please tell me what's happening."

Finally, the truth came out.

It's true. Your voice has poisoned him. That I cannot deny any longer. And the only thing that will heal him is your voice. Your human voice. In order to save him . . .

"I have to be changed. . . ."

Yes. But what's more is that you have, in essence, found a siren in him. The lack of his voice is killing you, too.

I shook my head. "How is that possible?"

I cannot explain how two souls join. No man or element or god ever could. But you are tied to each other. Because of that—because of your true, consuming, pure love—you will thrive together . . . or you will perish together.

305

"I don't understand." I swallowed, trying to make sense of it all.

If he hadn't heard your voice, he'd be fine. But once he aged, however many years from now that might come, you would have found yourself deteriorating then. Or if you had disobeyed Me so fully that I had to kill you, he'd have died in the same breath. You are tied through your souls. Now, what happens to one body happens to the other. And since your voice has taken hold of him, killing him slowly, you fall down with him. Slower, of course, as you are still Mine. But it will consume you eventually, all the same.

Instantly, my thoughts went to Aisling. I felt an immense guilt for betraying her secret now, but there was no way to hide it anymore. Because, if this was happening to me, shouldn't it have happened to her? Shouldn't she have weakened when Tova died?

But then, it wasn't simply Tova, was it? She'd followed her grandson and then her great-granddaughter. I smiled a little, seeing the glitch in this mysterious bond between sirens and the ones we loved among the living. Her love wasn't singularly focused, and as a new generation of the family she made exist thrived, she blossomed with it.

"You lied to us," Elizabeth roared. "You knew!"

I didn't believe such a thing could be. How could anyone love you as I have? More than I have? How could two people from

306

such different worlds connect without words? I knew you could have passing affairs and comfortable acquaintances. I thought I gave you so much, there was no room for any other love.

"There's always room for love," Padma whispered. "Even if it's as small as a crack in a door."

Our eyes met, and I remembered saying those very words to her in New York. How could I have known what they would eventually mean for me?

I gave her a sad smile. "It's true. I found a way. I love him, and it's killing us both." I covered my mouth, but there was still nothing left in me to cry.

"This isn't your fault, Kahlen," Mlaka insisted.

I nodded my head. "But it is. It would have been one thing for us to fall in love. Maybe we would have felt each other's sadness or happiness from time to time, maybe my body would have floundered fifty years down the road when his did. That all would have been fine." I paused, needing to catch my breath. "But I let him hear my voice. I poisoned him, and that's killing us."

I am sorry. If only I had kept you from fleeing from Me, perhaps you would never have found him again.

"It was always going to happen." My lungs were working overtime, unable to handle the strain. "Think of everything we've done. All the places we've been, eras we've lived through. How often have you run across someone more than once?" I demanded of my sisters.

307

They were all silent. My breathing slowed, leaving me with an empty feeling.

"More and more, I think he and I were destined to be together. And if all we had was that one, perfect day, then I'm happy to die with that in my heart." I shook my head. "It's *his* life I hate sacrificing. I've dealt out so much death, it's fair for it to come for me. But for him . . . he's just so . . . so . . ."

There wasn't a good enough word for him. *Decent* implied that he only met the bare minimum of politeness in life. *Kind* didn't cover the deep down affection he carried at all times for other people, even when he was sad. Even *perfect* wasn't fair, because he was certainly flawed, and those shortcomings, that humanness, made me love him all the more.

"We know." Miaka rested her head against mine without actually putting any weight on me.

I swallowed. "I don't think I can talk anymore. My voice is tired."

"Of course it is," Miaka said lovingly. "You've given every last piece of it. I mean, the only way . . ."

No.

"But you just said—"

I know what I said. But we can still have more time. Her body is stronger than his.

Elizabeth suddenly understood the conversation. "Why

are we even debating this? He can save her and she can save him. You need to let her go."

I could be wrong. What if she is changed back and her voice does nothing? What then?

"Then she'd still have the last few days or hours of her life with the person she loves."

She won't remember him. For all we know, this could make everything worse.

Elizabeth, broken, all the fire in her body burned out, shouted fiercely at the water. "How could it possibly be worse?"

It would be worse for Me!

Though no human could have possibly heard, for us, Her words echoed in the cavernous sky, shaking the trees and causing rocks to tumble.

She had no eyes, could produce no more water than She already had, and still we could all feel Her crying.

I am isolated. I cannot have equals. You are all I have, and you avoid Me if you can. I understand why. I know you hate what you're forced to do. Have you ever once tried to imagine how it feels to be Me?

"We understand Your burdens! We do!" Miaka assured Her. "We carry them, too."

No, you only feed Me. I slave, unnoticed, unthanked. It is rare that any of the girls who serve Me give Me a second thought any time I don't call for you. Is it too much to hold on to one of you who does for as long as I can? When you all leave, I'm less than a memory. I'm not ready to be forgotten.

I swallowed, feeling conflicted and beloved. My soul mate and I were ending the other's life with our absence, and at the same time, the thought of leaving the Ocean without my companionship felt cruel.

Miaka's sympathy carried into Her, and we all felt it in return. "Think of the pain You just felt as she remembered her only love. Would Your hurt be greater than that? Maybe. But consider, Kahlen did that. She left. She did what we're asking You to do, and she did it for Your sake."

The Ocean stilled, seemingly unmovable. I refused to let myself feel hope at Miaka's suggestion. Even if it was true, there was no way to get me back to him.

Padma, who'd been detached from everything, wiped at her eyes and quietly approached us. She stuck her hand in the tiny, lapping waves, her expression hesitant.

"Kahlen told me that You could be the mother I deserved."

And I could!

"But You threatened to kill me. That's a notch above what my real mother did, but that doesn't encourage me to love You."

But I love you! You're all precious to Me.

"Then please," Elizabeth begged, "stop pushing us away with Your anger."

310

How else am I to get your obedience? It's already precarious as it is.

Elizabeth hung her head. "I have always been a little defiant. I can't not be that girl. But we are not all Ifama or any of the others You've had to do away with. We chose to stay. We're still here."

"And had You spoken with us like this years ago, You would have had a handful of daughters eager to be with You." Miaka held tight to me as she spoke, and I could feel her hope radiating.

I could hardly focus on that, though, for the Ocean wept and wept, so lost by Her own misunderstanding of us, the very things She'd created. My feet were still in the water, but I lowered my hand as well.

"Don't think I won't somehow miss You," I promised. "If I'd lived long enough to change back in seventy years or if I die tomorrow, don't think I wouldn't hold on to You."

I will ache for you. Every day, I will.

"I know. But when I'm dead, You'll have the others. They understand now."

And soon they will go.

"But not until they've taught the new girls to love You as we do."

"I'd stay longer," Miaka said.

I peeked over, smiling up at her.

She gave a little shrug, seeming bashful to make the admission. "I would. I'm happy here. I'm happy with You."

"I could stay longer," Elizabeth offered. "Every family needs a rebel. Let's be honest, You'd be bored without me."

There was a tiny glimmer of joy in the midst of Her sadness.

Padma joined in. "You know what my life was before You. I'm in no rush to run from You."

"We could promise to add Kahlen's time onto our own if You want us to," Miaka said, glancing at Elizabeth and Padma for their approval. They both nodded.

"We'll take on what she owes You," Elizabeth said. "We're happy to."

I dug my fingers into the gritty rock, feeling like it was the only way I could hold Her hand, trying to assure Her that She had never truly been alone. There was an air of stillness about Her, as if She was taking us in, building Herself around a new truth.

I promised you that your voice would never be his undoing, that his death would never come at My hand. This wasn't how I thought it would unfold, but the only way to show you how much I love you would be to keep this promise. It's all I have left.

Her thoughts swirled, aligning into action.

You all will have to do the planning. I assume we'll need to do the change near Maine. I will bring you there when you're ready.

"I'll take care of everything," Miaka vowed. "I'll leave as little to chance as possible."

Go now. I need to prepare.

"Will You be all right?" I asked.

I must be. Go, dear girl. This is all I can give you. Now you can finally know how I love you.

31

The first thing I was aware of was hunger. It felt as if my stomach had caved in on itself, and the lack of food was painful. And even as I considered the ache, it felt foreign, as if pain was something meant for other people, not me.

Then I felt myself rocking. I was moving, but it was dark, and I didn't know where I was or how I was being transported. I wasn't using my legs. My legs, all of me in truth, felt wasted. Like I couldn't use them even if I had to.

"Hello?" I managed. My throat burned, that painful scratch of swallowing salt water. It took all my energy to lift my head.

I could see how I was moving now. Three girls were carrying me, two cradling my body, and one supporting my legs.

"Where are you taking me?" My voice was weak and shaking.

As I asked the question, I realized there were bigger unknowns. I couldn't think what my name was. Ellen? Katlyn? Neither of those sounded right in my head. I didn't know where my family was; I didn't know where they ought to be. I couldn't even think of names or faces, but I sensed I had lost something or someone.

My breath began coming fast as fear took over. My instinct was to run, but I could barely keep my head up.

"Please don't hurt me."

No response.

As we came toward a house, I started wondering if this was my final destination. Lights were shining out through the windows, and while it filled me with a sense of warmth, I didn't trust that feeling. I groaned as they walked me up to the porch, though they moved slowly and smoothly, trying to keep the steps from jostling me. The girl to my right, an Asian beauty with hair as black as the clothes she was wearing, nodded her head three times, and they all lowered me in unison.

I was left propping myself up on my elbows, breathless from the move.

"Where are we? What do you want?" I whispered hoarsely.

The girl at my feet, another beautiful goddess, looked sadly to the others, then at me, as if I were failing a test.

"I'm so confused," I whimpered. "Please, what's going on?"

The final girl, wild haired and gorgeous, pointed to the house.

"Is this my home?"

She made a face, unsure how to answer. The Asian girl touched my arm to get my attention. She nodded.

As if she was losing something, she touched my cheek. Her hand felt damp. The girl at my feet pushed her hands flat together as if she was praying and bowed once. The final one ruffled my hair and smiled.

Wordlessly, they rose and ran around the corner of the house.

"Wait!" I called as loud as I could. "Who are you? Who am *I*?"

I started crying, terrified. What was I supposed to do now?

My noise must have alerted someone. The door opened wide, the bright light blinding me.

"Kahlen?" a man said. "Julie! Julie, get over here, it's Kahlen!"

"Help," I pleaded. "Please."

"Oh, thank goodness!" cried a woman, coming to the door. "We thought you were dead."

"Doesn't look far off," the man muttered under his breath.

"Hush! For goodness' sakes, Ben. Help me get her inside."

He lifted me from the ground, taking me inside his house. He gently lowered me onto a plush chair.

"Sweetheart, where in the world did you go? Akinli's been worried sick. We all have."

The woman—Julie—pulled a quilt off the back of the couch and draped it over me while she placed her fingers on my wrist and watched the clock.

"Who?" I asked in a hoarse whisper, grasping for the blanket. There was a pause, a mix of shock and sadness covering their faces. "I'm sorry. Can I have some water?"

Ben rushed back to the kitchen, and Julie crouched down beside me, tucking me in better.

"Kahlen, do you remember me?"

I shook my head. "The girls told me this was home, but I don't know you."

"What girls?"

"They didn't say. They ran."

"Here you go," Ben said, coming around the corner with a glass.

I pushed myself up and gulped it down, desperate for water. "That helps." I touched my head, trying to keep my thoughts straight.

"She doesn't remember anything."

Ben huffed. "Well, at least you can talk this time," he said cheerfully.

I squinted. "What?"

Julie pressed her fingers to her lips. "I don't know how to explain any of this to you."

"Maybe Akinli should," Ben offered.

"I doubt he'd have the strength."

"Pshh," Ben mocked. "For her, he'd find it."

Julie made a face, allowing the truth of that. "Can you walk?"

"I don't think so."

"It's okay." Ben came over, gently placing his arms beneath me. "I've gotten pretty good at this."

Julie went ahead of us up the stairs, and it was such a narrow path, I had to lean my head into Ben's shoulder. She led us to the end of the hallway, knocking gently on the door. The light was dim, and I heard something humming in the background.

"Hey. How you feeling?" she asked sweetly.

"You kidding?" someone teased lovingly. The voice sounded as worn as I felt. "I could run a marathon."

Something stirred in my chest. It was as if I'd been

holding my breath underwater and my lungs just realized I'd broken the surface.

She laughed. "You have some company. Up for it?"

The person took a breath, and it rattled a little on the way in. "Sure."

Julie nodded to Ben, and he walked me into the room as Julie pulled up a chair for me.

"Thank you." I tried not to moan as I hit the seat. Ben lost his balance and wasn't as gentle as he meant to be.

I finally made eye contact with the boy in the bed. He lay on his side, a tube in his nose and another in his vein. His cheeks were sunken, and his skin was ghostly pale. His hair might have been blond, but it was fading into a gray, making it hard to tell. The only part of this boy that held any life at all were his eyes, which brimmed with tears when he saw me.

"Kahlen?"

I sat still. These three people all called me by the same name, which sounded sort of like Katlyn and Ellen and made me believe that maybe they actually knew me.

"Where did you go? Where have you been? I thought you were dead." His chest worked overtime, trying to keep up with his mouth, spilling over with words.

"Can you get her a pen? Please?" He lifted an arm weakly. It was all bone. "I just need to know."

"A pen?" I asked.

Once again his eyes lit up.

"You can talk?"

I stared at this boy, at how he was overjoyed at one of the most basic things a person could do. "So it would seem." I smiled.

He flopped onto his back, laughing from his gut, and based on Julie's tears, I was guessing she'd been waiting a long time for that to come back.

"I've been dreaming of that sound." He stared at me, seeming so content just to have me in the same room. "I'm so glad you're safe."

I looked at him and the other two people whose names I'd just learned. "So . . . so this is home then?"

Akinli looked at me, perplexed, then turned to Ben and Julie.

"She said some girls left her here and told her it was home. That's all she knows. She doesn't even know you." Julie wiped at her tears, trying to calm herself.

He moved his eyes back to me as quickly as he could manage. "Kahlen? You remember me, right?"

I stared into this face, searching for something familiar. I didn't recognize the angle of his chin, the length of his fingers. I didn't know the slope of his shoulder or the shape of his lips.

"Akinli, right?" I asked. This poor boy. I pitied him in the depths of my heart. Clearly, he'd already been going through something, and I could see the last scrap of fight he had in him dying with those words.

"Yes."

"I don't remember ever seeing you before in my life. I'm sorry."

He pressed his lips together as if he was swallowing the urge to cry.

"But," I said, "I know your voice. I know it as if it were my own."

Akinli, this strange boy whose life at the moment seemed to be hanging on this, pushed himself from the bed.

Julie gasped, watching as his arms trembled under his weight, even as thin as he was. He crushed his eyes together in concentration, willing himself up.

I heard Ben whisper to himself, "Come on, come on, come on."

When Akinli, breathing as if he truly had just run a marathon, was fairly close to upright, he held out an arm for me.

I fell into it fearlessly.

We leaned into each other, neither of us strong enough to stay up on our own.

"I thought I'd never see you sit up again," Julie cried.

We both turned to her, smiling at the happy tears on her face.

"I'm feeling okay, all things considered," Akinli said.

"All right, let's not push it." Ben came over and helped him lie back down.

I felt a little better. There was still a buzz of confusion in my head, but I was welcomed here, and Akinli's voice was nourishing me better than food would.

I sniffed as a few tears escaped, lifting my hands to wipe them away. It was then that I caught the only clues I'd been given by whoever had left me here.

On one wrist someone had written *You are Kahlen*. The other said *He is Akinli*.

I flipped my hands over and searched up and down my arms, hoping there was more.

"Look," I begged, holding out my arms.

"Pretty handwriting," Ben commented.

Julie hit him, but in a way that seemed playful. "Seriously?"

"That's all you have?" Akinli asked.

"Apparently. So, all I know is who I am and who you are." I looked into his eyes, the glowing blue, and sensed that was all that mattered.

EPILOGUE

The doctors called it a miracle. Day by day, the illness that had crippled Akinli was fleeing his body. It had been replaced by an enthusiasm for life and a desire to make up for lost time.

Though no one had diagnosed me, I knew I was healing from something myself. My road to wellness was shorter than his, but it was no less astonishing.

Akinli became the only history I had. He told me how we once danced by a tree while others watched with envy. He wowed me with a story about a beautiful dress I had that turned to dust in the guestroom, leaving a white stain on the hardwood floor. And he told me about our first kiss, how it was beautiful and disastrous at once, and how every kiss since then held the same strange magic.

I listened to it all, etching the words on my heart. For as much as I studied these stories, I never understood how our paths crossed the way they did. I could only conclude it was fated.

When we'd all settled down from that first night, Julie found a bag on the porch, which we thought must have been left by the same three girls who had brought me to them. Just like the clues on my skin, I'd only been left with two worldly possessions. The first was a wad of cash that I immediately handed to Ben and Julie as compensation for giving me a home. Most of it went to pay for Akinli's medical bills, which was fine with me. I didn't know if there was a word bigger than *soul mates*, something that meant the feeling of being so connected that it was hard to tell where one person ended and the other began. If there was, that word belonged to Akinli and me.

The second thing was a bottle of water. It was so peculiar, this water, a blue that was both dark and brilliant, too thick to see through but still carrying light. No matter the season, it was always cold, and there were tiny shells in it that never settled.

Sometimes I slept with it, even though it was cold enough to wake me up if I rolled on it the wrong way. It was the only clue I had to tell me who I had been before the night I was left on the porch, and I loved it second only to Akinli.

Somehow, I knew that this love was important, as if treasuring the water meant I treasured myself. And I did. I loved my recovering body, I loved my blue-eyed soul mate, I loved my adopted family.

I held the water to my chest, and I loved.

ACKNOWLEDGMENTS

On all my acknowledgments pages, I take the time to thank God, my family, and the various teams of people who make my books happen. While my love for Christ never fades, and I am still eternally grateful to the many people in my life who allow these stories to exist in print, forgive me if I move in a different direction this time.

Right now I want to specifically thank my readers. Just you.

This is the first book I ever wrote. And this is the book that made me know I wanted to write forever. And this is the book that didn't originally make it through the traditional publishing route. The only reason this is in your hands now is because you all cared so much about what I eated that it got a second chance. You did that.

A solid 90 percent of my readers are teenage girls. You are a force. You influence art and fashion and culture. You're eight different kinds of cool. You get overlooked far too much, but my seventeen-year-old soul loves you endlessly.

And to the handful of you who are dudes or adults or actual puppies or something, high fives for loving what you love without shame. Sometimes books written specifically for young adults or for a female audience don't get a lot of credit. Thanks for not caring and picking it up all the same. That matters to me. Lots.

I would write even if I couldn't share what I made. I am a storyteller and hope I get to do that always. But the only reason these books are on shelves is because you wanted them to be. That is awesome. And though I can't list all your names here, that doesn't make them any less valuable than all the ones I could.

Keep making things happen. Thank you forever.

—K